Joseph Bennett

Letters from Bayreuth

Descriptive and critical of Wagner's Der Ring des Nibelungen. With an appendix.

Joseph Bennett

Letters from Bayreuth
Descriptive and critical of Wagner's Der Ring des Nibelungen. With an appendix.

ISBN/EAN: 9783337386696

Printed in Europe, USA, Canada, Australia, Japan

Cover: Foto ©Andreas Hilbeck / pixelio.de

More available books at **www.hansebooks.com**

Letters from Bayreuth

DESCRIPTIVE AND CRITICAL

OF

WAGNER'S
"DER RING DES NIBELUNGEN"

WITH AN APPENDIX

BY

JOSEPH BENNETT

(Special Correspondent of the "Daily Telegraph")

LONDON: NOVELLO, EWER AND CO.

MDCCCLXXVII.

G

NOVELLO, EWER AND CO.,

PRINTERS,

69 & 70, DEAN STREET, SOHO, LONDON, W.

WISHING TO DEDICATE THIS LITTLE BOOK TO

A VALUED FRIEND

AND

AN ACCOMPLISHED MUSICIAN,

THE AUTHOR HERE INSCRIBES THE NAME OF

ANGELINA GOETZ.

PREFACE.

WITH two exceptions the "Letters" which make up this book originally appeared in the *Daily Telegraph*, in 1876, and are reproduced with the consent of the proprietors of that journal, to whom the author's warmest thanks are due.

As an excuse for their presentation in a collected form, it may be urged that, at this distance of time, no other English writer is likely to follow the example of the German, French, and Italian critics by offering to his countrymen a permanent record of an interesting artistic event. Conscious of his ability to deal with the great theme only in an inadequate manner, the author would gladly have surrendered it to any one of the able colleagues who were with him at Bayreuth.

The Letters, written from day to day during the performance of *Der Ring des Nibelungen*, have not been retouched, and are therefore a statement of first impressions which, however erroneous, may at least claim the merit of genuineness.

LONDON, *May* 1, 1877.

INTRODUCTORY.

NEXT month the eyes of the entire art-world will be directed towards the little Bavarian town of Bayreuth, watching the production, in a series of performances three times repeated, of Richard Wagner's crowning work, *Der Ring des Nibelungen*. Some difficulty may arise in ascertaining the whereabouts of the place, and far more in imagining an adequate reason for its choice as the *locale* of an event with which, *per se*, it has no right of association. Here, however, Mr. Edward Dannreuther, a competent authority and guide on all matters Wagnerian, steps in. "Bavarian Bayreuth," he tells us, "is a charming, quiet old town, with a literary and social past by no means despicable, healthy, prettily situated, easily accessible, and in the very centre of Germany." But the place seems to have been chosen more for what it is not than for what it is. " It has no regular theatre," continues Mr. Dannreuther, " and consequently no theatrical or fashionable public, no leading newspaper, political, clerical, or literary; its negative credentials, in a word, are perfect. Then why not Bayreuth ?" Why not, indeed ? if it be necessary to isolate the ultimate manifestation of Wagner's ideas from the active life of the day. We are assured that "the trilogy is as little

B

fit for the miscellaneous public of a fashionable watering-place as for the subscribers of a Stadt or Hoftheater; and as its performance, in any case, must partake somewhat of a private nature (a sort of family feast which the musical *élite* of the world prepares for itself), it appears obvious that the less such an undertaking comes in contact with certain equivocal elements of public life in great or fashion-able towns the better for all parties concerned." I cannot argue this with Mr. Dannreuther, but may venture to point out that, if Wagner's art-work is to be "of the Future," its manifestation must not be limited, like the preaching of John the Baptist, to desert places. No doubt a good many Pharisees and some unbelieving Sadducees will find their way to Bayreuth next month, with a chance of bap-tism to the new faith, and unquestionably the imagination is struck by the idea of a perfected music-drama born in a place which has, in a distinctive sense, neither politics, religion, literature, or art. Yet needs must, some time or other, that it encounter the conditions of life in the great world; and the sooner we learn that, though conceived with-out reference to such a result, it is compatible with those conditions, the higher will be our estimate of its value. But whether or not a need existed for going into the Bavarian wilderness with the *Nibelungen*, nothing could be done without a theatre specially built, and wholly devoted to long and elaborate preparation by artists called

from all points of the compass. Even a slight acquaintance with the *Nibelungen* proves this; nor is it more
difficult to understand why Wagner wished to get away as
far as possible from the ordinary operatic atmosphere.
Years ago he declared that the lyric drama, then and now
accepted as such, had succeeded in making "the mob
fastidious, the upper classes vulgar, and the entire body of
spectators vulgarly fastidious duffers." To all these considerations the fact is due that the Art-Work of the Future
will be unveiled to the *élite* (with a proportion of Pharisees
and Sadducees) in a special theatre, near an obscure
provincial town, inhabited by people who don't read
newspapers and know nothing of art save what may be
learned from wandering practitioners.

It must not be supposed by those who have just heard
Tannhäuser for the first time, and lately made acquaintance with the word *Nibelungen,* that the Bayreuth performances are the result of a sudden fervour. As a matter
of fact, we go back twenty-five years to the earliest
announcement of their inception, since which time the
idea has been kept in view with the patience and resolute-
ness characteristic of all those by whom great things are
done. It was in 1847 that the master turned his attention
seriously to the Nibelungen myth as a subject for lyric
drama, and not long afterwards a poem entitled "Siegfried's
Tod" was finished and in the printer's hands. Wagner

himself tells us, however, that, so far, he had no practical object in view. " I planned and carried out my poem of ' Siegfried's Tod' "—so writes he in a "Communication to his Friends "—" simply to satisfy an inward impulse, and in no way with the idea of producing it on our stage, with its existing theatrical appliances, which I could not possibly help considering unsuitable to the purpose. It was not until very recently that there was awakened in my bosom a hope that, provided certain circumstances turned out favourably, and after a certain time, I might be in a position to bring this drama before the public, but not, however, till after the successful results of certain pre-parations destined to prove, as far as possible, that the performance would be effective. This is likewise the reason of my still (1851) keeping back the poem. At the period in question—namely, the autumn of 1848—I never thought there was any possibility of producing the piece; I looked upon its poetically-technical completion, and the attempt to carry out musically certain parts, merely as a source of inward satisfaction which I gave myself at a time when I was disgusted with public affairs, and had drawn back from them." The " inward impulse " to which Wagner here refers did not cease its action with the finish of " Siegfried's Tod." Partly because the charm of the ancient Teutonic epic grew upon him, partly through the influence of an idea by-and-bye to be spoken of, Wagner began to see the possibility of a masterwork unequalled of its kind in point of dimensions. The immediate result was another poem, "Junger Siegfried;" but still his view expanded, and, finally, embraced that which the world is soon to know by more than report, as the three dramas of *Der Ring des Nibelungen*, with an introduction, *Das Rheingold*. More than this, there dawned upon the master the hope of presenting his great work at a special festival. To conceive the idea was, with him, at once to make it known, and in the "Communication" already quoted we read : " I intend presenting my myth in three complete dramas, which a grand prelude will precede. With regard to these dramas, though each one is certainly to form an independent whole in itself, I have no intention of writing any 'stock-pieces,' according to modern theatrical ideas, but have resolved on the following plan for their representation : I propose producing, at a festival got up at some future time expressly for this purpose, the three dramas with the prelude in the course of three days and an introductory evening. I shall look upon the object of the performance as completely attained if I and my artistic companions, the actual representatives, succeed in conveying artistically my aim to the real intelligence of the feelings (not critical intelligence) of those spectators who shall have assembled to become acquainted with the said aim. Any further consequence is as much a matter of indifference to me

as it necessarily appears superfluous." The approaching
representations at Bayreuth embody, therefore, the aspirations, and are destined to crown the labours, almost of a
lifetime.   To them Wagner has been looking for nearly
thirty years, and, whatever their result, they will command
the respect due to unflinching resolution and patient labour,
in union with a lofty purpose.   How sternly these qualities
were exacted by circumstances can be shown in few words.
It was not till the early months of 1856, two years after
the completion of the Nibelungen poem, that Wagner began
setting it to music; but he laboured so earnestly that in little
more than a year he had finished "Das Rheingold," "Die
Walküre," and a portion of "Siegfried." Then trouble set
in, taking the form of despondency arising from a conviction
that the work would never see the light.   So powerful was
this feeling, that only when the King of Bavaria accorded
Wagner his patronage in 1864 did he again address himself
to the herculean task.   Meanwhile, he had composed
Tristan und Isolde and *Die Meistersinger*—works better
adapted to the resources of the German stage, and calcu-
lated, as events proved, to strengthen popular feeling on his
behalf.   Once more, however, there was delay.   Wagner's
presence in Bavaria raised a storm before which he retreated
to Zurich, and the Nibelungen Festival seemed again far
off.   But the darkest hour is that which immediately pre-
cedes the dawn, and the dawn began in this case with an

idea started by Carl Tausig. Tausig was a fit champion of Wagner—a man who, like Siegfried, would go through fire to win the Brünnhilde of success—and he actually set about discovering a thousand Germans willing to lay down £45 each in order to carry out the festival project. It is scarcely necessary to add that he failed, or that he died in 1871, leaving the outlook seemingly as dark as before. But the idea of the gifted and regretted pianist survived him, starting into full activity when the fact dawned upon some shrewd mind that forty-five subscribers of £1 each are just as good, financially speaking, as one subscriber of £45. Here was the key to success, and, forthwith, Wagner Societies arose on all hands and in many countries. Money poured in, necessary arrangements were hopefully made, and, writing last month, Mr. Dannreuther was able to say: "The theatre is built and paid for, stage arrangements and preliminary rehearsals completed; in short, all expenses defrayed up to the present day, and a balance in hand of upwards of 15,000 florins." Upon the whole undertaking, we are told, there must needs be a serious loss, foreseen from the beginning; but the fact only increases our admiration of the pluck which, through years of discouragement, has at last attained the wished-for end.

The theatre, which now stands close to Bayreuth, is not the least noteworthy feature in a remarkable enterprise. It has been described as "a solid structure of red brick and wood, neither beautiful nor ugly, without the slightest attempt at architectural show, but exactly fit for its purpose." So far, it is by no means unique, but the interior arrangements are altogether so as regards the "auditorium," which is intended to accommodate less than 1,500 persons. The peculiarity of this part of the building consists in the fact that there are neither side boxes nor side galleries. Every seat faces the stage, and only those in the end gallery are raised above the level of the floor; the object being, apart from any question of convenience, to secure the invisibility of the orchestra, which Wagner has stationed down in a pit. His theory is that no executive apparatus should come between the spectator and the drama—no gesticulating players upon instruments, no bâton-waving conductor, no orchestral lamps, and no prompter's box. All these are stowed away out of sight, while such parts of the house as command a view of them in their present position are purposely left tenantless. Nothing, therefore, will disturb the scenic illusion of the stage, between which and the audience comes only a screen of orchestral music; rising from its source in the pit, and colouring whatever is seen through it with hues of sensuous beauty. Strange to say, the idea of such a theatre is not new, though as far as Wagner is concerned it may be original. A correspondent of *Le Guide Musicale* points out that it occurred to Grétry long before the birth of the composer of *Der Ring des Nibelungen,* and was thus expressed by the French master : " Were I a manager, I should say to my architect, ' Recollect that what we here want is not a monument constructed solely to be looked at and to produce a grand effect on the eye; the essential point is that we may be able to hear perfectly all that is said upon the stage. . . . No boxes, small or big. I would have a circular house, all rising in steps ; each place convenient and separated by slight lines of demarcation an inch high. After the orchestra for the musicians a series of steps should form a single circular amphitheatre, gradually rising, with nothing above it save a few trophies painted in fresco. The orchestra should be veiled from view, and neither the musicians nor the lights of their music-stands should be seen from the side of the audience. The effect would be magical, and we know that in all cases the orchestra is never supposed to be where it is." Save that Wagner's auditorium is wedge-shaped, and that of Grétry circular, the agreement of the two designs is perfect—so perfect that we find it easier to believe in Wagner borrowing from his predecessor than in any accidental coincidence.

I come now to the artistic principles which in *Der Ring des Nibelungen* Wagner definitely illustrates. These, I may assume with confidence, are but little understood outside the limited circle of enthusiasts who have made their study a close pursuit; and the fact arises, not from any reticence on Wagner's part in expounding his meaning, but from the involved, turgid, and wordy fashion in which he writes. Ordinary readers, even of a careful and, as far as possible, lucid translation—that, for example, which appeared in the *Musical World,* from the pen of Mr. J. V. Bridgeman, five years ago—soon grow weary of trying to fathom an explanation needing itself to be explained, and as a result the vast mass of those into whose hands musical literature passes have but a hazy notion of the matter at issue. In saying this I do not judge Wagner harshly. Rather do I accept his own estimate of himself; for in his " Communication " we read, " How painful this kind of intercourse [addressing his 'friends' by pamphlet] is for me I need not, probably, assure those who know me as an artist; they will themselves perceive it from the style of my literary works, in which I must worry myself in the minutest particulars to express that which I would fain give concisely, lightly, and glibly in the art-work itself. . . . . So hateful to me is this literary business, and the necessity which has compelled me to turn author, that, when writing this 'Communication,' I hope I appear for the last time as a literary man before my friends." Apart from the fact that Wagner was destined still further to " worry " himself and others by a form of expression neither concise, light, nor glib, I cannot but regret, for the master's sake, that his hope failed. But leaving this point, let me try to give, in language as clear as the subject allows, some idea of the theories now actually in process of manifestation.

First of all, it is necessary to clear the ground of a notion that the Nibelungen " stage plays " make any pretensions to be regarded as operas—in other words, that, appertaining to the same class as *Don Giovanni* and *Fidelio*, they invite judgment as an advance upon those masterpieces. If it can be established that no such pretensions are raised—that, in point of fact, Wagner now brings forward a new thing, to be estimated for itself alone, and not by comparison—a huge difficulty is at once removed, and the question becomes liberated from a great deal of encumbering matter. On this point let Wagner himself speak, in a sentence the significance of which cannot be overrated: " I write no more *operas*, and, as I can invent no arbitrary name for my works, I call them *dramas*, because 'by my doing so I at least most clearly define the standpoint whence what I offer must be accepted." These words, penned in 1851, deserve at the time now present most careful consideration, and should have their just weight recognized. In view of them, that which we know as opera retires from the field. It is, of course, open to any man to say, looking at *opera* on the one hand and Wagner's *drama* on the other, that this or

that confers the greater pleasure, just as he may choose a
peach before an apple or an apple before a peach. But it
is no longer possible, in the sense of being fair and true,
to take opera into consideration when estimating the
merits of the new music-drama. Wagner has a perfect
right to insist upon this, and to say : " Here is something
evolved from my artistic consciousness by an independent
process ; it is not subject to any existing laws, because
constructed without the smallest reference to them ; and I
demand, therefore, a judgment on its merits." The result
is that, while we are entitled to reject the music-drama if
it do not satisfy us, we are debarred from abusing it
because it fails to coincide with something else. For my
own part, I gladly recognize the distinction Wagner lays
down. It enables me to approach the Nibelungen dramas
as M. Ollivier went into the German war—with a light
heart, and to accept them, if I must, without violence to
the affection entertained for other things, seeing in the
art-work they illustrate an addition to sources of pleasure,
not a substitute for any one of them.

It is important to observe further, while I am on the
negative side of the question, that Wagner expressly
repudiates the charge of being a conscious iconoclast.
Popular opinion represents him as a fanatic image-breaker
who, having forced his way into the sanctuary of art,
furiously smashes everything his axe can reach. "This

character," writes Wagner, "which they consider themselves bound to attribute to me, haunts the brains of most
of the musical critics when they do me the honour of
referring to me. Since they never trouble themselves
about the *whole*, it is, in the first place, only *details*
respecting form which can constitute for *them* the subject
of reflection, and the blame of their having to reflect with
regard to music they lay upon me, who advance towards
them with reflected music. Then, again, simply because
they have only *the musician* before them, they confound
me with certain hair-splitting, actual, absolute musicians
who—as such—can still make a show of producing works
of imagination only by the arbitrary variation and trans-
position of the form. In their grief at my destroying
the musical forms which were the salvation of established
custom, they go so far as to regard as a misfortune in store
for them any work that may be announced by me, getting
so excited that they even actually imagine that my operas,
though utterly unknown to the managers, are inundating
German theatres. So absurd does fear render people."
Elsewhere Wagner explicitly states : " It was not by any
means on principle, and as a reflecting breaker of forms,
that I proceeded to the destruction [Wagner must mean
'proceeded to ignore,' for he has not destroyed] of the
aria form, the duet form, or any other usual operatic form;
but the omission of those forms resulted quite as a matter

of course, entirely from the nature of the subject, the portrayal of which in a manner intelligible to the feelings,
and by the expression necessary to it, was the sole thing
about which I cared." On the strength of his own words,
then, let me take Wagner out of the false light which gives
him an unreal hue, and truthfully formulate him thus :—

1. He is *not* a writer of operas, but of dramas, to which
music is subordinately allied for particular purposes and
under special conditions.

2. He is *not* the active enemy of musical forms, but
simply one who cannot use them in the task upon which
he is engaged.

Now we are on firm ground, and see clearly what is
before us. We approach, untroubled by lines of communication with extraneous matters, Wagner's finished work,
and regard him not as a destroyer to be assailed for doing
violence to things consecrated by great genius and universal worship, but as a creator, who invites our suffrages
to place that which he has made upon some vacant pedestal
in the Walhalla of art. At the same time, none of us can
forget that, if Wagner be not, as he declares, an iconoclast,
the distinction is sometimes hard to draw, and the fact
that most people think otherwise arises from his own
behaviour. Bitter words, the pouring out of contempt and
scorn, may result from an irascible condition of mind, but
the world cannot always discern between the consequences

of momentary weakness and the expression of deliberate conviction.

Passing now to what Wagner is and does, as distinct from what he is not and does not, and premising that the intention is to be expository, not critical, I must first point out that the perfected music-drama claims judgment as a whole. It has already been seen how much contempt Wagner pours upon those of his critics who view him as a musician only, instead of as a producer of works whereto both poetry and music are essential. He complains, in fact, of being regarded as an ordinary opera-composer, for whom some *littérateur* has saddled and bridled a verbal hobby that he might "witch the world with noble horseman-ship." Making no pretensions to such a character, Wagner demands that his works shall not be judged solely from the musician's point of view. He stands forward, in fact, as the mixer of a compound, having three ingredients, all necessary though not all co-ordinate—poetry, music, and stage representation. Over the third I may now pass as not affecting the important question raised by the nature of the union between the first two. Wagner starts with the idea that the object of dramatic representation is to excite the imagination and arouse emotion. To this end musical language—exclusively the language of sensation—is a direct means. But music is incapable of going beyond purport. It cannot precisely define the object of the sensation. " The necessary extension and expansion of the musical linguistic expression consist, therefore, in the acquisition of the power of portraying, with recognizable sharpness, the Individual and Special, and this power musical language can acquire only by a union with verbal language." Thus words and music appear as the complement of each other. Without the first the second is vague; without the second the first is weak. But we make a mistake by supposing that the necessary union can be arbitrarily effected. While, on the one hand, music must ally itself only to what is similar in verbal language, there must be in the verbal language a yearning for a real sensual expression of feeling. The existence of this yearning is the mark of fitness for the work the tone-poet has to do, and the stronger it is " the more decidedly does the subject require an expression which the language of tone only can supply with suitable copiousness." It follows from this that the musician will choose his subject with reference to its power over his emotions—in other words, with reference to fitness for human expression; while the music to which he allies it will be the natural outcome of the feelings it has excited. It follows also—I am reproducing Wagner's own argument, *bien entendu*—that the word-tone poet will seek his subject where he is likely to find it most purely and intensely human. He has to deal, as Wagner says, with the " Purely Human, freed from all Conventionality," and hence we find the author of *Der Ring des Nibelungen* turning his back upon everything in the nature of historico-political life to seek his materials among the myths and fables of antiquity, which can be dealt with from an emotional and imaginative standpoint, at pleasure. Wagner did not discover the necessity of this course till he approached the story of Frederic Redbeard, with a view to its dramatico-musical treatment. Then he found out that such themes are not musical, and that they entail the subjection of the poetic faculty to minor and unworthy considerations. Abandoning Frederic Redbeard, he approached Siegfried—the " Purely Human, free from all Conventionality "—and found himself, he observes, " in a perfectly new path, struck out by me with unconscious necessity—a path in which, as an artist and a man, I advanced towards a new world."

It is curious to observe with what earnestness Wagner insists upon his subjection to an " unconscious necessity." By such means was he driven to the unfettered humanity of the *mythos*, and by such means, when there, were the nature and form of his musical expression determined. He admits doing nothing as a matter of choice, but everything as a logical result from which there was no escape. The force of this law influenced him in the rejection of established musical forms, but the result was arrived at

c

only by slow degrees. How the change at length came
about he has told us in his usual elaborate fashion, the
gist of the argument lying in the subjoined extract:
" The fact of involuntarily knowing the traditional form
still influenced me so much in my *Flying Dutchman* that
every person who attentively examines the piece will
perceive that the form frequently guided me in the arrangement of my scenes ; it was gradually, first with *Tannhäuser*,
and then in a more marked degree with *Lohengrin*—that is
to say, as I gained a clearer insight into the nature of my
subject and the mode of portrayal requisite for it—that I
entirely shook off the influence of form and regulated the
representation more and more decidedly only by the requirements and peculiarity of the subject and situation."

We have now arrived at the main bases of Wagner's
theory, and may define them in set words, as thus :—

1. An intimate union of poetry and music for the
production of an effect which neither can create alone,
and for the purposes of which each is subjected to
a condition, viz., the poetry 'must' be that only which
"yearns" for musical expression, while, on its side,
the music must unreservedly adapt itself to the
requirements of the poetry. But, inasmuch as in
this union the generative power belongs exclusively to
poetry, then—

2. There can be no question of submission to arbitrary

musical forms, which, indeed, lie outside of the matter altogether, and possess no title to recognition.

Subordinate to these general principles are others of great importance to Wagner's scheme of a perfected music-drama. It is well known that his later works are mainly based upon a few distinctive themes, identified with the leading persons and situations. Wagner tells us, in an interesting way, how this characteristic feature arose. Before the *Flying Dutchman* was composed, he had written and set music to the ballad for Senta, now found in Act 2, that ballad being "a condensed picture of the whole drama." Afterwards the musical picture thus made expanded over the drama, and, says Wagner, "I had merely to develope according to their respective tendencies the various thematic germs comprised in the ballad to have, as a matter of course, the principal mental moods in definite thematic shapes before me. When a mental mood recurred, its thematic expression, also as a matter of course, was repeated, since it would have been arbitrary and capricious to have sought another *motivo* so long as the object was an intelligible representation of the subject and not a ' conglomeration of operatic pieces.'" But now as to the formation of the themes themselves. At the outset of his career, Wagner adopted the traditional melody, seeking originality by means of harmonic and rhythmical artifice, as in *Rienzi*, where he employed the Italian-French style of Spontini. In the

Flying Dutchman he advanced towards the Folks-melody, with its sharp rhythms and buoyant animation, but he found that this was only applicable where the subject touched upon national elements. As, however, he was determined to have no more to do with ordinary operatic tunes, "unconscious necessity" obliged him to seek melody in the feeling delivery of the language. But here he found himself hampered by the melodic poverty of modern verse, which, according to Wagner, has a fancied, not an actual, rhythm. So situated, he was bound either to follow the verse and write music wanting in rhythmics, or, having invented a rhythmic tune, to engraft it artificially upon the poetry. Wagner adopted the first course, making up for deficiency of rhythm by what he styles a "harmonic animation of the expression," and by a more and more characteristic accompaniment of the orchestra—a plan fully illustrated in *Lohengrin*. There still remained, however, the need of finding out some way of rhythmically animating the melody out of the verse; and to this discovery Wagner's guiding star led when it pointed out Siegfried as a subject. In this hero the master saw "man in the most natural and most joyous fulness of his sensually-animated manifestation; no historical garb any longer circumscribed him; no relation arising from without at all impeded him in his movements, every one of which was so regulated, out of the inmost source of his love of life, that error and confusion, nourished in the wildest play of the passions, could be heaped up all around him to his evident destruction without his having for one moment, even when face to face with death, checked the inward source in its welling stream outward, or considered aught as possessing authority over him and his movements, save the necessary outstreaming of the restlessly-bubbling inward fountain of life." To put modern verse, with its "indistinct bodiless form," into the mouth of such a splendid being was impossible, and Wagner asserts that the subject would have been altogether abandoned had he not discovered, where he found Siegfried, a perfect linguistic expression. This was the alliterative verse of the old Scandinavian and Teutonic poets—" a verse in which the people themselves once wrote poetry, when they were still poets and myth-creators." An example of this will be more instructive as to its form and texture than any amount of description, and I give, therefore, an English imitation and translation, by Messrs. Magnússon and Morris, of the last verse in the "Lay of Sigurd" (*Siegfried*), as found in "The Story of the Volsungs and Niblungs:"

"Much have I spoken,
    More would I speak,
If the sword would give me
    Space for speech;
But my words are waning,
    My wounds are swelling—
Naught but truth have I told—
    And now make I ending."

It is in verse thus nervous, emphatic, and rhythmic that Wagner has written *Der Ring des Nibelungen*, and this alone, he contends, satisfies the requirements of the music-drama.

We have now followed Wagner along his course to the point where he stands at present, and seen how, from a perception of the principles upon which verse and music should be allied, he passed to the evolution of melody from the spirit of verse, and then to the adoption of that form of verse which, in his view, best aids musical expression. Apart, then, from the fundamental principles stated above, the Bayreuth performances illustrate—

I. The excellence of the myth as subject-matter, because dealing with a humanity evolved, so to speak, from the national life, and free from all entangling associations.

II. The spontaneous melody growing out of a feeling delivery of the words.

III. The value of the ancient alliterative verse as lending itself to the purposes for which music and poetry are associated.

Here my preliminary task ends.

"DER RING DES NIBELUNGEN."

BAYREUTH, AUG. 12.

MR. DANNREUTHER is quite right in insisting upon the negative qualifications of Bayreuth as a place for the Wagner Festival Stage-Play. It is itself a negation, and a stranger may wander long about the streets without coming into contact with anything suggestive of the living, active, and positive world, unless, indeed, he encounter a big Bavarian soldier. Of all dull towns I imagine Bayreuth, in its normal state, to be the dullest. Moreover, the utter sluggishness of the place has its impression heightened by plentiful signs that, once on a time, there was life here. In the fine old days when Germany grew princes wholesale, Bayreuth had its little court and was a little capital. The potentate whose sway it owned called himself, I believe, a Margrave, and contrived, somehow or other, to keep up a considerable state. He built palaces, whereof two stand in the town, and, though used for a variety of purposes, are decaying with a fit air of dignity. The third, some two miles off, serves to perpetuate the memory of its builders, much as the Brighton Pavilion immortalizes our own George the Fourth. But these edifices are by no means the only signs of Bayreuth's dead-and-gone grandeur. The place abounds in fine old houses; its streets are adorned with some very respectable statues—that, among others, of Jean Paul Richter, who lived and died here—while numerous fountains are continually pouring out streams of clear water. These fountains, by the way, are a distinctive feature of the town which they serve to ornament as well as to bless. Of course they trace their origin to the Margraves, and the question at once arises why it was that the tyrannous old German princes expiated their bad ways by providing so much water. Once on a time they built churches, but the logic of that course is clear enough, and, unless they saw in the "pure element" a symbol of the "mystical washing away of sin," I cannot account for the fountains. The Bayreuth churches, let me add, are not remarkable, and it is to be feared that the Margraves cared very little about them. On the whole, the town has a stately and dignified look, but is wofully faded. It is a tenth-rate Versailles, crossed with a sleepy provincial borough. Sleepy! I should think so, indeed! Even now, when the place has been galvanized into prodigious activity, one can easily distinguish Bayreuthers from strangers. The native and his favourite beast of draught, the ox, are well matched, both going dreamily through life at the slowest possible pace, and with a constant disposition to lie down and ruminate. Just now, as I have said, Bayreuth is uncommonly alert, having actually two things on its mind at once—making money in abundance out of the strangers within its gates, and spending a little economically in decoration. The first of these operations Bayreuth will certainly carry out with success, and, as regards the second, a convenient decision has been arrived at to the effect that there is something exhilarating in the appearance of the fir which chances to abound on the neighbouring hills. The result is that Bayreuth has a fir eruption out all over it. Great branches, stuck in the ground to resemble trees, line the pavements—or rather the space where pavements should be—festoons of fir cover the fronts of the houses, and wreaths of the same cheerful material, made more lively by paper flowers, are stuck wherever room can be found for them. Adding to this a crowd of poles, from which in due time—for the Bayreuther is careful of his bunting—flags will fly, and it must be granted that the inhabitants, considering their normal sleepiness, have bestirred themselves to some purpose, even though, like John Gilpin's spouse, they do not overlook the value of " a frugal mind."

The most conspicuous figure in Bayreuth life just now is made by the strangers who swarm all over the town and are contemplated by the natives with placid wonderment. They are certainly worth contemplating, as being a remarkable crowd of curious people. Let me frankly say that never before did I see so many short-sighted folk, with long hair and "loud" hats, gathered together in one place. The ambitious literary youth of England used to imagine an intimate connection between genius and the Byron collar, but they had a model which these Wagnerites lack. Why, then, is it that faith in the "Art-Work of the Future" goes in company with spectacles, long hair, and funny head-gear? I confess I cannot tell. There must be a reason, else hardly would the phenomenon manifest itself in men who have come from all points of the compass and have nothing in common save their faith. An eager race are they, and a splendid contrast to the slow Bayreuther. You may see them flying along the road that conducts to the Wagner Theatre, "larding the lean earth," à la Falstaff, as they go. Or you may see them dart off towards Wagner's villa, there to be outer-court worshippers; for the master does not indiscriminately "receive." Or you may see them racing about the streets, stopping suddenly whenever some fresh manifestation of Wagner is made by a shop window, which means stopping every few yards, for upon the man who has given Bayreuth fame Bayreuth, in turn, bestows whatever it can of honour. The whole town is, so to speak, given up to him, and you see him everywhere. In photographs and statuary, on pipe-bowls and tobacco-boxes, on toilet ornaments and album covers—on countless things, indeed, appear the well-known face and form. Nor is this all. Wagner's music floats about the streets. Here a soprano may be heard declaiming at the top of her voice some passage from the *Nibelungen;* here a tenor, and there a bass, labour hard and lustily; or, perhaps, a violinist has got up among the harmonics, or a pianist is hammering out a succession of "diminished sevenths," which clash against each other in their search for a key never to be found. Whatever the music may be, it is in the "Ercles' vein," and the performer cultivates passion. I declare to you that I have not yet heard in Bayreuth a single quiet melodic phrase. Music, here and now, is nothing if not "sound and fury"; nor do musicians deserve the name unless they rave and roar. Well, these are times when the world lives fast and has sharp emotions.

I have already referred to Wagner's house—"an eligible residence standing in its own grounds," and one which points to the fact that a musician "of the future" need not be prepared, as a matter of necessity, to sacrifice the present. Let me confess to looking upon this, the master's chosen home, with anything but complacency. One is glad, of course, when genius meets with the reward of life's good things. It rarely does so, because, perhaps, adversity supplies better nourishment; but in the exception we recognize that which is fitting. There is, however, about Wagner's state a pretentious, theatrical air such as a man of taste must regret to see. A house decorated with gaudy frescoes and mottoes, bearing a fantastic name, and surmounted, as now, by three tall poles, from the top of which stream three large flags—such a place I can associate with genius only by a severe wrench. *De gustibus*, &c., of course, and nobody has a right to complain, however sorry one may be that such vanities give pleasure. But Wagner was never chargeable with failing to exhibit his light in all sorts of ways and places. He strives to keep himself before the world, and if he attract passing attention by decorating his house, he is, at least, consistent. Though the house and the theatre be wide apart, in this respect they are very close together indeed. Pass we, then, at a step, to the edifice in which, for three weeks to come, Wagner will exhibit his perfected music-drama. The site has been well chosen, some half-a-mile beyond the skirt of the town, and on the top of a gentle eminence which itself is backed by a wooded hill, crowned with a round tower. Rather a pretty way runs thither, the tree-shaded road being flanked by corn-fields and gardens, while the little terrace in front of the building commands an interesting view of the quaint old town and the hills beyond—a view none the less German because the most prominent object in the foreground, next to a lunatic asylum, is a big brewery. Some attempt has been made to lay out the meadow through which the carriage way passes to the theatre as a pleasaunce, but at present the trees are small, the walks ill-kept, and the grass rough. Roughness, indeed, is characteristic of the whole affair, for, to say nothing of the wooden houses flanking the main building, and devoted to refreshment, the theatre itself seems to have been hastily thrown up, and its courses of red brick left innocent of "pointing." Of architectural beauty the exterior has none whatever. The object was utility, and, this gained, nothing beyond was sought. In time to come, perhaps, when funds are plentiful, the artist as well as the builder will have to do with the place, and succeed in making it less of a disappointment than it is now. As with the exterior, so elsewhere. On entering the auditorium, one sees a perfectly plain room, suggesting a college lecture hall on a large scale. It is in the form of a parallelogram, the stage occupying the centre of one of the long sides; the side opposite being devoted to a gallery for dis-tinguished visitors (called the Princes' Gallery), having another for less remarkable people above. The area seats rise tier above tier from the brink of the space occupied by the orchestra to the level of the Princes' Gallery, so that every seat faces the stage, and commands a full view of it. As the seats spread out like a fan from below upwards, it is obvious that there must be a large vacant space along the shorter sides of the parallelogram. The effect of this is, however, broken by a division into bays, separated by Corinthian columns supporting entablatures. Over these entablatures and around the pillars are placed the gas lamps—few in number, because during the performance the house is kept in darkness save for the light reflected from the stage. As the roof is low, and the distance from the stage to the opposite side not great, one is struck on entering with the apparent smallness of the place. In a little while, however, the width of the auditorium asserts itself, and it is possible to believe in the accommodation of some 1,500 people. Regarding the arrangements behind the curtain I cannot speak, but the working of the stage at the rehearsal on Wednesday night was so perfect that reports of admirable ingenuity may be credited without reserve. The rapidity, silence, and smoothness with which the various changes were made contrasted most favourably with the uproar and clumsiness which theatre-goers are so often called upon to notice, while the absence from view of all such executive machinery as orchestra, prompter, and foot-lights made the drama intensely real to the audience, who seemed indeed to be " assisting " at it in a very forcible sense of the term. This then is, in brief, the Wagner Theatre as it awaits the revelations of the Wagner drama.

While I am writing, Bayreuth is busier than ever at the work of decoration, and from my window I behold several citizens in a condition bordering upon animation. The phenomenon is due to the expected arrival of the Emperor William, which event will come off in two hours' time. Strangers meanwhile are pouring in, many of them to drift helplessly about in search of a resting-place either not found at all or only bought with much gold.

BAYREUTH, AUG. 13.

A KAISER does not come to Bayreuth every day, and it must cheerfully be granted that the inhabitants made very respectable, and unwonted, exertions to give Emperor William a fitting welcome. Not only did they dress their streets and houses with the plentiful fir, but managed to achieve a display of flags which would have done credit to Gravesend what time some popular Princess passes through that river gate. The Bavarian colours — blue and white—were, of course, plentiful, and so were the black, white, and red of the German Reich. Of other national flags I saw none, not even the Union Jack, which, considering the swarm of English now here, might have been shown, if only as a matter of courtesy to stranger guests. The Emperor arrived on Saturday afternoon, and his progress through the town to the fantastic palace called the Hermitage was a triumph. I am not sure that it is needful to give minute particulars of an event which, if

memorable for the Bayreuthers, was not in itself remarkable, nor shall I inflict upon you a list of the Royal and
other dignities who came with or immediately after their
Imperial chief.   Enough that the distinguished visitors
were so numerous that the officials, whose full evening
dress grew more and more dusty as the day progressed,
were kept on the alert till a late hour.   As a matter of
course, the Emperor was serenaded by torchlight, but, as
the Hermitage is some miles away, you must take the
imposing effect of that ceremony upon trust, and not from
my description.   This I can answer for—that Bayreuth
did not go to bed till eleven o'clock; and, as it is usually fast asleep by ten, the sense of dissipation and of
" making a night of it " which generally prevailed may be
imagined.   But, if Saturday was a great day, what shall
I say for Sunday, when, at an early hour, the popula-
tion, strengthened by crowds from all the country round,
descended into the streets, and kept those usually deserted
thoroughfares in a state of commotion till midnight?   Bayreuth, like Marguerite decked with the jewels, must have
doubted its own identity, and asked with puzzled surprise,
" Can this be I ? "   But the day was one of puzzles all
round.   The provincial folk from the hills and plains
walked about in wonderment, staring hard at Wagner's
painted villa.   Bands of youths in wonderful braided caps,
and decked with mysterious insignia, furnished strangers

with matters of curious inquiry; while, as train after train brought hundreds of fresh arrivals, the question of what was to be done about food and lodging became more and more a riddle. The spare house-room in a town of 18,000 inhabitants is necessarily limited—and limited, I am obliged to say, most of us found the commissariat yesterday. At hotels people begged a meal in vain, and it was only after a hot and dusty walk to the huge *restauration* adjoining the Wagner Theatre that a reasonable prospect of restoring exhausted nature opened out. However, the day wore on, and, as the blinding, brilliant sun drooped in the west, all Bayreuth poured itself along the road to the ugly temple from which is to shine a new light upon German Art.

The scene in the neighbourhood of the building became really animated and picturesque towards seven o'clock, at which hour the performance of *Das Rheingold*, the prologue to *Der Ring des Nibelungen*, was announced to begin. From the terrace the eye commanded a long stretch of the thronged highway, and of the flag-decked town beyond, while near at hand were assembling the component parts of such a gathering as the art-world rarely sees. A polyglot gathering it was, and to move about amongst it gave one an idea of the confusion that must have prevailed at the foot of Babel. English, French, German, and Italian were mixed up in jabbering confusion, but in the minds of all, I will venture to say, there was often

a single thought: "This is a great day for Wagner." A
great day, verily—so great that it is easy to imagine the
master looking back incredulously upon the time when, as
he somewhere says, with a half-humorous sense of degradation, he " made pianoforte arrangements of Halévy's
operas." Let us think what we will about Wagner's
theories, let us detest his music as we may, and entertain
what opinions we choose as to the means he has adopted
to assert both, there is no getting away from the fact that
through long years of opposition or indifference—laughed
at by some, treated with silent scorn by others—he has
persevered, till now a great nation, headed by its Emperor,
sits at his feet, and the whole civilised world, moved by
curiosity or admiration, gathers round. The qualities
necessary for such a career are no ordinary ones, and I
am very sure that the most hearty opponent of Wagner's
principles was yesterday generous enough to sympathise
with his amazing triumph.

But while we are gossiping thus on the terrace, the
gaily dressed crowd are moving quickly into the theatre,
and the road yonder has become lined with people waiting
to see the Emperor and his companions pass. Now, too,
a trumpeter advances, and blows a phrase from the
Götterdämmerung by way of signal that places should
be taken. Let us obey. When at length Emperor,
Princes, and Mightinesses of various orders have also seated

themselves, what an audience is gathered in front of that mysterious curtain! Were there at our elbow some timely informant who knows all, he might say, passing over the exalted personages with whom everybody is acquainted, "Yonder is Liszt, as the representative of modern German music, and around him are hundreds of his fellow-countrymen, who are also his fellow-artists. It is true we do not see Heller, or Brahms, or Raff, or Volckmann, or Joachim; but German art is here in mass, if some of its heads are wanting. America has sent Laing from cultivated Boston. Yonder is Hanslick, of Vienna, most terrible of thrusters at the joints in Wagner's harness. Filippi, of Milan, is not far off; Albert Wolff, of Paris, sharpens his pencil above us; from England have come Benedict, Randegger, Davison, and a score others." But we do not want to be told this. We are assured, without such details, that Wagner is now to be tried by a very special jury indeed—men of eminence gathered from every land, to command whose notice is in itself an honour. There is little time for personal observation. Hardly have the occupants of the Fürsten Gallerie taken their places before the gas is turned down, sounds are heard from the concealed orchestra, and a peremptory command for silence runs round the house.

It will hardly be news to say here that Wagner prefaces the three dramas of *Der Ring des Nibelungen* with an

introduction in one long act, called *Das Rheingold.*
This work, the music to which was composed at Zurich
as long ago as 1856, has been some years before the world,
and is well known in Germany. Nevertheless, in the
hearing of the English public it must be spoken of as a
new thing; and first with regard to its bearing upon the
rest of the story. The central idea of Wagner's great
drama—regarded, at all events, as a source of action—is
the pernicious influence of a talisman which, originally
conferring upon its owner the gift of power, has become
connected with a curse. In the *Rheingold* we witness,
so to speak, the birth of these influences, and the first of
the results destined to be continued "to the bitter end"
in the body of the work. The prologue introduces us to a
strange world. We are among the fantastic creations of
Teutonic mythology. Gods and giants, water-maidens,
imps of the nether regions, and all manner of fabled wonders pass before us. Of the real world we see nothing. It
is a region of fancy, where anything may happen, and
where, as a matter of fact, many things do happen of a
very strange and terrible sort. Wagner tells us that the
true materials for a national music-drama lie here. If so,
I can only marvel that pantomime-writers have been so
long unconsciously hovering on the verge of a great discovery. Let me describe the scenes and incidents exhibited on the stage of the Wagner Theatre last night.

When the curtain rises, after a few bars of undulating music on a pedal bass, we are looking at the depths of the Rhine, through which float Woglinda, Wellgunde, and Flosshilde, the Rhine Daughters who there watch and ward a certain golden treasure. Presently comes up from the depths below a dwarf, Alberich the Nibelungen. Seeing the Rhine Daughters, he is enamoured of their beauty, and makes love to them after his fashion, they meanwhile playing off upon him as much coquetry as though they were daughters of earth. The game having been carried on till the dwarf burns, as he says, " with lust and rage," a diversion arises when brighter rays from above reveal the gold. Alberich asks what it is, and hears that measureless wealth and power will belong to the man who shapes a ring from the metal, but that he only can do it who forswears love. Exasperated with the sportive maidens, Alberich fulfils the condition, seizes the gold, and disappears. The next scene reveals a stately castle in the distance, and, in the foreground, Wotan and Fricka asleep. Moved by dread of coming doom, Wotan had engaged the giants Fafner and Fasolt to build this stronghold, offering as a reward the beautiful goddess Freia. On awaking he is reminded by his wife of the bond, but rests content with an assurance that the subtle fire-god Loge will enable him to evade it. Presently Freia enters, appealing for help against the giants, who have come to claim their reward. Wotan temporises with them. Other gods enter upon the scene, followed at length by Loge, who, having his own purpose in view, tells of the wealth which Alberich enjoys, and of the power of the ring he has fashioned. The giants' cupidity is thus excited, and they offer to accept the gold and ring in payment. But, as Wotan declines to give what belongs to another, they depart carrying with them their prize. No sooner is Freia gone than the gods, whose perpetual youth her fruits had sustained, begin to grow old. Alarmed at this, and yielding to entreaty, Wotan agrees to accompany Loge in a raid upon Alberich's ill-gotten booty. Now we are introduced to a subterranean cavern, aglow with fire, filled with clouds of steam and noisy with sound of hammers. This is Alberich's domain, the power of the ring making him master over the horde of Nibelungen workers. One of these, his brother Mime, has fashioned a tarn-helm, which enables the wearer to assume any form, and he would fain use it himself, but, with blows and curses, Alberich takes it from him. Presently, as Mime lies writhing on the ground, Wotan and Loge enter, to hear through him of the tarn-helm; upon which the fire-god forms his plan. Alberich returns, hunting a troop of his slaves, and is instigated by Loge to show the tarn-helm's power. First he assumes the form of a huge snake, and next that of a toad, on which Wotan instantly puts his foot, and Loge

seizes the helm. Alberich at once resumes his proper
shape, but is bound fast by the gods and dragged upwards
as a prisoner. We are now on the earth's surface once
more, and see Alberich haled from below by his captors,
who insist, as the price of liberty, upon the hoarded gold.
This having been brought by the Nibelungs, the tarn-helm
is next demanded, and at last the ring also, Wotan tearing
it from the dwarf's finger amid cries and imprecations.
Then the captive is released, but as he limps away he
attaches to the ring a curse for its possessor :—

> " To death under forfeit
> fear shall have hand on his heart;
> through length of life,
> day by day he shall die;
> so serve the ring,
> though he seems its lord."

Now the giants return with their pledge (the gods resum-
ing their youthful look when Freia enters), and demand
as ransom gold piled before Freia till she is hidden. All
is surrendered, but her hair remains visible, and Fafner
demands the tarn-helm. Then Fasolt, seeing the light of
her eye through a chink, insists on the ring as a stop-gap.
But with this Wotan will not part, and the giants are
about to take Freia away, when the goddess Erda, rising
from the earth, solemnly warns Wotan to yield the cursed
thing. Reluctantly he consents; the giants receive the
ring, and at once suffer from its bane. Quarrelling over

a division of the spoil, Fafner strikes Fasolt dead, packs up the booty, and departs. Now the gods can take possession of their castle. Donner summons a thunderstorm, and on its clearing away a rainbow bridge is seen thrown across the Rhine, over which Wotan and the rest pass. while the Rhine Daughters are heard from below lamenting the loss of their treasure. Then the curtain falls.

Reserving observation upon this part of the legend till the whole can be discussed, I pass to the music with which Wagner has sought, in his own peculiar fashion, to illustrate it. Though with scarce so much rigidity as in the later portions of the drama, Wagner here acts upon the principles which have been already described. We have in *Rheingold* the continuous flow of formless music, the vocal phrases supposed to grow naturally out of the verse, the characteristic *motivo* associated with each personage, and the rich orchestration that never ceases to pour over the whole a flood of musical colour. Each of these features produces its own result. The formless music streams along the mind, so to speak, without passing into it. Speaking generally, we are not drawn to a consciousness of its presence, since it offers but little of an intelligible character to lay hold of. That it works upon the emotions in harmony with the drama—assuming that such a fantastic story touches us at all—cannot be denied. Wagner's music intensifies the poetic beauty of his dramatic subject when it is beautiful, and also makes its ugliness more pronounced when it is ugly. This is no doubt his object, and he would say that the thing must not be judged alone, but in association. Here, however, the question arises whether an art so perfect in itself is exhibited in a proper light when degraded to the condition of a mere reflector of often unworthy things placed in juxtaposition with it. The vocal phrases in *Das Rheingold* may grow naturally from the verse in the consciousness of their composer; but no one else can be expected to recognise the fact, or discern the natural necessity for their unvocal character. Rarely, indeed, do we come upon a passage that can strictly be called melodious, and, for the most part, the ear has to endure the musical equivalent of " bald, disjointed chat." As to the characteristic *motivi*, ingeniously varied though the manner of their presentation be, they soon become wearisome. The trick is not an exalted one, and Wagner works it without mercy. His redeeming point lies in the orchestration, which, from first to last, is marvellous in its skilful use of every resource. It requires some resolution to turn from the drama to music having no meaning by itself; but, limiting attention to Wagner's orchestra, the connoisseur enjoys a rich treat. Beautiful ideas, ingenious devices, and constant variety are found there in phenomenal abundance. Such are the general impressions derived from last night's work — impressions further experience may modify, it is true, but which at present raise very serious doubts whether the new music-drama has the smallest chance, apart from Wagner's personal influence, of achieving popularity.

Referring to the performance, it may be well to begin by stating the exact composition of the orchestra. There are in this wonderful and most perfect machine thirty-two violins, twelve violas, twelve violoncellos, eight double basses, four flutes, four oboes, one English horn, three clarionets, one bass clarionet, four bassoons, one contra-fagotto, seven horns, four tenor and bass tubas, three trumpets, one bass trumpet, four trombones, one double-bass trombone, one double-bass tuba, eight harps, and the usual number of drums. As may be imagined by connoisseurs, this orchestra is, above all, rich in the volume and majesty of its bass, the "sixteen-feet tone" brass and wood instruments helping to produce effects of the highest grandeur; but at the same time the balance is as perfect as anything can be. As for the unity, precision, and delicacy of its playing, one can easily suppose that the finest artists of Germany, under such a conductor as Hans Richter, and with unlimited opportunities for rehearsal, leave nothing to desire. But, as a matter of fact, the Wagner orchestra does more than meet bare requirements; it oppresses the ear and mind, so to say, with a sense of full and ripe perfection. Difficult though the music be, the tide of sound rolls on with unbroken smoothness, reflecting lights and shades with infinite delicacy from its surface; while the fact that it streams upwards from a hidden source impresses the imagination to an extent not dreamed of, perhaps, either by Wagner or by Grétry before him. Whatever may come of the festival in other respects, we now know fully what an orchestra can do, and where in a theatre it should be placed. The leading characters were well sustained by Frederike Grün (Fricka), Marie Haupt (Freia), Lillie Lehmann, Marie Lehmann, and Minna Lammert (Rhine Daughters), Franz Betz (Wotan), Heinrich Vogl (Loge), Carl Hill (Alberich), and Carl Schlosser (Mime). Wagner is his own stage-manager, and leaves but little to the option of artists; but the ladies and gentlemen named above must be credited with carrying out his ideas admirably. Nothing was done on the stage without a purpose; and the bearing of each god or goddess had a distinctiveness as marked in. its way as the theme which represented him or her in the musical department of the work. Praise should especially be given to Herr Vogl (Loge), whose impersonation of the old-world Mephistopheles was throughout admirable in a very high degree. The one drawback associated with all this excellence lay in the fact that very few of the artists could be called singers. Much

of whatever vocalism once existed on the lyric stage
in Germany has disappeared before the advance of
mere declamation, and the fact is here vividly—sometimes painfully—illustrated. But as Wagner's phrases
are more often declamatory recitative than melodies, the
want of vocalism cannot be looked upon as at all a fatal
defect. His artists, moreover, have frequently to make
themselves heard through such an orchestral din that
singing would avail them little. They must either shout
or scream, and they do it. Notwithstanding many
rehearsals, there were several blunders in the working of
the scenic department, and I am told that these exasperated Wagner to such an extent as to make him leave
the theatre. But the mistakes, though regrettable, inter-
fered little with success. Regarding the scenery itself,
I cannot say that anything astonishing was presented
to an English eye. The *coup d'œil*, however, was often
wonderfully beautiful, and some of the devices were bold
and novel in a high degree. The bed of the Rhine
presented a charming picture, although the floating of
the Rhine Daughters seemed a little too mechanical, and
wanting in freedom. More striking yet, perhaps, was the
subterranean abode of the Nibelungs, into which we all
appeared to descend, while steam hissed fiercely out a
welcome. Nothing could have been more happy than the
idea of introducing steam to give reality to the glow of

reflected fires and increase the grimness of the place. Praise was also deserved by the grouping and management of the crowd of Nibelungen over whom Alberich tyrannised. In fact, the entire scene was a masterpiece. Later on, the coming up of the storm summoned by Donner, with the lightning and thunder attending it, made a strong impression; but, on the other hand, the management of the rainbow bridge over the Rhine to Walhalla did not satisfy expectation.

BAYREUTH, AUG. 14.

"DIE WALKÜRE," the first part of the drama proper, was given last night, and it is necessary to begin this letter by showing the connection of the story with the events of *Das Rheingold*. A considerable interval of time is supposed to have elapsed, in which Wotan, ever impressed with a sense of coming danger to the gods, has not been idle. No respecter of the marriage tie, he has associated with Erda, the Earth-goddess, who has borne unto him a band of nine warlike maidens (Walkyries) destined to single out the noblest warriors slain in battle and convey them to Walhalla as defenders of that stronghold and of the gods. But above all has Wotan remembered the Nibelungen ring, now possessed by the giant Fafner, who guards it in the form of a monstrous

"worm." Unable himself to seize it, because unable to
break faith, Wotan longs for the talisman as a means of
defence against the enemies of his order; and he has
conceived the idea of producing a hero sprung from his
own race, but independent of the gods, and therefore
not able to compromise them, who shall get possession
of the prize. For this purpose he has lived amongst men,
and had a son, Siegmund, and a daughter, Sieglinde, to
the former of whom he has destined a sword, Nothung, now
buried to the hilt in the stem of an ash around which is
erected the house of Hunding, a warrior whom Sieglinde
has married. At the opening of *Die Walküre*, the brother
and sister have been separated from their youth, and
Siegmund, a disarmed man, flying from enemies, is
unconsciously approaching Sieglinde's house, the rude
interior of which we see when the curtain rises to a
stormy orchestral accompaniment and to the roar of
thunder. The apartment is empty till the fugitive enters
and sinks exhausted upon a couch, where Sieglinde finds
him and ministers to his wants, without recognition taking
place. Soon are they mysteriously attracted to each other,
and Siegmund remains in the house till Hunding returns
from an expedition against the very man who now enjoys
his hospitality. Here, also, no recognition ensues till
Siegmund relates his adventure, upon which Hunding tells
him that he is safe for the night, but that in the morning

they two must do battle. Husband and wife then retire, but as Siegmund muses upon his condition and upon the mysterious attraction of his hostess, she returns (having given her husband a sleeping draught) to hold further talk with the stranger. Their mutual sympathy at once developes into passionate love, which the discovery of close relationship does not check. In rapture Sieglinde points to the sword no man has yet been able to draw from the ash-stem, and Siegmund at once releases it. Then she exclaims, " in highest ecstasy," " Thy own sister winn'st thou at once with the sword," while Siegmund answers, " Bride and sister be to thy brother ; so blossom the Walsung's blood." Here the curtain quickly falls. For the present I refrain from comment upon this extraordinary scene, passing on to the second act. Amid a wild rocky region we find Wotan, conscious of the impending fight, despatching Brünnhilde, a favourite Walkyrie, to guard his son. As she goes away to arm, Fricka enters, and, in her character as protectress of the marriage tie, insists that Hunding shall be avenged. Wotan excuses the act of Siegmund and Sieglinde ; but, as the result of a long altercation, the god gives his word that Siegmund shall fall, and Fricka triumphantly drives away. On Brünnhilde returning, equipped for the mission, she hears from the desponding Wotan the whole story of his devices to stay the doom of the gods, but that, nevertheless, the hero

Siegmund must die. Brünnhilde protests that she will not help the deed, and Wotan leaves her with words of warning against the thwarting of his will. As she retires, Siegmund and Sieglinde appear, the woman conscious of her shame and full of self-reproach. Exhausted at last by emotion, she faints, and then Brünnhilde stands before the doomed hero to tell him of coming fate. Siegmund defies her, but eventually his distress at leaving Sieglinde so works upon the war-maiden's feelings that, heedless of Wotan's command, she promises to guard him in the fight. A storm comes on, Hunding's challenging horn is heard, thunder peals, and Sieglinde revives to find her brother gone. But presently the lightning shows him to her, and to us, on a ridge of rock, in conflict with Hunding, while above floats Brünnhilde as protectress. The maid is not, however, to work her will. Another flash reveals Wotan on the side of Hunding, with outstretched spear, against which Siegmund's trusted sword shivers at the moment that his enemy deals a fatal blow. Brünnhilde has fallen back before Wotan, and now, descending to the lower ground, places Sieglinde on her horse and rides away. At a wave of Wotan's hand Hunding falls dead, and the curtain comes down as the god threatens vengeance against the flying Brünnhilde. The third act opens amid rocks and caverns, where Brünnhilde's eight sisters meet, some returning through the air with the bodies of slain heroes over their saddle-bows. Presently the ninth war-maiden appears, bearing Sieglinde from the pursuit of Wotan. She appeals to the rest for protection; but they are horrified at her disobedience, and refuse. At this juncture Sieglinde asks to die as a release from trouble. When, however, Brünnhilde reveals the secret of her coming maternity, she as ardently wishes for life, and hesitates not to wend her way alone towards the sheltering wood in which Fafner guards the ring, taking with her, as the war-maiden's gift, the splinters of Nothung. Now comes Wotan thundering along in storm. At first the sisters try to hide Brünnhilde, and next they plead for her; but the god strikes her name out of the roll of the Walkyries, and proclaims her banishment from his face for ever, condemning her, moreover, to lose her divinity and to sleep on the rock where they are till a man shall wake her and claim her for wife. A touching scene follows, but the god will only concede that no coward shall have the maiden—that she shall be guarded by encircling fire through which faint heart cannot pass. Much moved, Wotan takes a tender farewell, and, kissing her eyes to sleep, lays her down, helmeted, mail-clad, and covered by her shield. Then, obeying his word, flames leap up to encircle the maiden, at whom Wotan takes a last look, saying, as the curtain falls, "Who fears to face the point of my spear will never pass through the fire."

E

Such is the story of *Die Walküre*, and who cannot see at a glance that it compares most favourably, in point of strong human interest, and even in circumstance and action, with the fantastic *Das Rheingold?* Who, moreover, cannot trace the influence of this fact in the music? Here Wagner had to deal with sentiments and situations highly poetical and deeply moving, which served to inspire him almost out of his own principles. It is true that the master never departs from the essential bases he has laid down; but very often, in *Die Walküre*, he approaches as nearly as possible to that which we commonly know as music, and in the degree in which he does so is the result beautiful. The whole of the first act is charming, simply because the *motivi* upon which it is built, even that representing Hunding, are true melodies. To these, though they are repeated incessantly, the ear turns with pleasure, above all throughout the long love scene for the brother and sister. We may be disgusted with impending incest; but when the door of the house flies open, revealing the silver moonlight beyond, and Siegmund begins, "Look how the spring laughs in the hall," we are carried along by a stream of sensuous music, glowing with luxurious colour, instinct with living melody, and in harmony with truest poetry, which takes possession of us and leads we care not whither. Here, at least, is a proof that, when Wagner pleases, he can produce that which is musically beautiful. If he would only remember that music, to be dramatic, need never be ugly, and that, for the sake of beauty, some departure might be made from the hard-and-fast lines of a theory, for how much more than now the world would have to thank him! In the second act, Wagner falls back upon the hard-and-fast lines in question, setting the dialogues of Wotan with Fricka and Brünnhilde to most terribly wearisome and painful sounds —for music it may hardly be called. The poor god drones on, and the orchestra drones with him, till the ear rebels, and excites the mind to a state of intense irritation. Happily relief comes when Siegmund and Sieglinde enter, and the entire act is redeemed by the solemnly beautiful music of the scene in which Brünnhilde warns Siegmund of his fate. Here again the charm is complete, though of a different order from that pervading the first act, and it is the more complete the more we recognise features which the masters share in common. Nothing could exceed the richness of the orchestration in this scene, or the perfect harmony between the musical and dramatic spirit. But the last act is the most remarkable of all. It opens with a chorus for the Walkyrie maidens which certainly has not its equal anywhere as an embodiment of wild, vigorous, rejoicing life. The music tells its own story, and as the voices rise one above another in strange exulting phrases, supported by the surging orchestra, we

want no interpreter of feeling or intention. This chorus
was received with a peal of spontaneous applause : and
it would be interesting to know how much of the tribute
arose from a sense of contrast to the monotony of a single
voice. In *Das Rheingold* there is no chorus at all (though
there are concerted passages for three voices), while in
Die Walküre we have only that of the war-maidens. Very
grateful, consequently, was the effect of the change, and the
shout of pleasure from the audience may in part be regarded
as unconscious homage to one of the most important
features in ordinary opera. I might dwell long upon the
beauty of the scene which embodies Wotan's farewell to
Brünnhilde, and discuss the tender expression of music
the effect of which is heightened by picturesque and
ingenious suggestiveness wholly beyond praise. But
enough that the drama closes in a manner worthy of its
opening, and leaves an impression not readily to be
effaced. A word for the orchestral writing must be added,
because in it lay the greatest source of pleasure. So rich
and satisfying were the instrumental passages in the
scenes where Wagner's theory allowed him to produce
beauty that the ear resented the intrusion of the voices
as an offence. "Let the orchestra alone," was the
instinctive command to the actors. Need this have been
the case? Is the negation of vocal charm a necessity of
the system?

With regard to the performance, little fault could be found beyond the general want of vocal skill. The cast was as follows: Siegmund, Albert Niemann; Hunding, Joseph Niering; Wotan, Franz Betz; Sieglinde, Josephine Schefzky; Brünnhilde, Amalie Materna; and Fricka, Friederike Grün. It should be added that among the Walkyries was Johanna Wagner, whose name English amateurs will specially recognise. Herr Niemann's voice was not at its best, but he played with entire spirit and propriety; while Herr Betz achieved prodigies among the strange progressions allotted to him in the distressing part of the second act. Sieglinde was admirably represented; but the chief honours fell to Frau Materna, whose Brünnhilde could hardly have been surpassed for gentleness and dignity. Of all the characters in the entire drama, Brünnhilde is the noblest, and of all the artists here present the one was chosen to play it who could best do it justice. Again the orchestra covered itself with glory. I may say, indeed, that this body of instrumentalists is a growing wonder, for connoisseurs are only beginning to appreciate its resources. The stage business was this time free from mishap, and, of consequence, its effects were good. Each act was applauded at its close, and the entire work made a deep impression.

BAYREUTH, AUG. 17.

As Wagner's great drama unfolds itself, and as the weather becomes, if possible, warmer, the expression of men's opinions on the artistic questions at issue grows more stormy. There are anti-Wagnerites here who, undeterred by the fact that they are a hopeless minority, stand to their guns like men, and make the various places of public resort so many battle-grounds. On Tuesday night, I am sorry to say, the conflict, from being one of intellectual give-and-take, descended to the region of fisticuffs, one of Wagner's followers, as pugnacious as his chief, taking the initiative. A Berlin critic having, within earshot of this personage —who represents the "Purely Human, freed from all Conventionality"—said something obnoxious about the *Nibelungen*, received a beer-can in his face, and had to retire with a broken nose. Something approaching a free fight is said to have resulted, and the Wagnerian champion found reason to know that society, for its own sake, insists, through a policeman, upon the "purely human" exercising a little self-restraint. Siegfried may have been a glorious hero when the earth was young, but the world, grown old and conservative of order, hales him before a magistrate.

The postponed performance of the second part of *Der*

Ring des Nibelungen took place last night, in presence of the crowded and remarkable audience who had already listened to the prologue and *Die Walküre ;* almost the only absentee, I imagine, being the Emperor William, to make up for whom, in point of numbers, at any rate, came the Austrian Premier, Count Andrassy. The production of *Siegfried* excited more than usual interest, because, unlike *Das Rheingold* and *Die Walküre*, it had never before been heard in public. Here was something absolutely new, though much of it was written years ago; and the army of connoisseurs settled down into their places, when the warning trumpet sounded, with a gusto plain to see.

Taking up the story of the poem as now further developed, I must remind the reader that at the close of *Die Walküre* the accursed ring remained in the possession of giant Fafner, who, as a huge lizard or dragon, watched it and the golden hoard. Also that Siegmund, the hero raised by god Wotan to recover the talisman, perished in fight with Hunding, and that his sister-wife fled into the forest, taking with her the hope of maternity. Between these events and the opening of *Siegfried* much has happened. The child of Siegmund and Sieglinde has been born, at the expense of the mother's life, which the attentions of Mime, the brother of Alberich and maker of the tarn-helm, could not save. Mime had met with Sieglinde in the forest,

and, knowing her story perfectly well, resolved to train
up the child as a means of winning the ring and
hoard for himself. The boy Siegfried has grown up
under his care into a splendid human animal, full of
intense life, and of vague aspirations and ideas which
Mime does his best to check. Matters are in this
condition when the curtain rises to show a huge rocky
cavern, fitted as part dwelling, part smithy, and opening
into the sunlit forest. Here Mime labours at fashioning
a sword for Siegfried, grumbling that he can never please
the "mannerless boy," who has a habit of smashing the
weapons at a stroke. To him Siegfried presently enters,
leading captive a huge bear, and mightily enjoying the
fright of the Nibelung dwarf. Dismissing the animal
after a while, Siegfried tests the brand Mime has made,
with the usual result, and then falls into .a moody,
discontented vein, abusing the maker with expressions of
extreme disgust at such companionship. He has found
out that the animals in the forest have more than one
parent, and wants to know who and where is the mate of
Mime, his supposed father. "I was thy father, and mother
as well," replies the dwarf; upon which he is called a
" lying old fool." Siegfried will not have him now as a
father, and proceeds to get at the truth by violence, with
such success that Mime not only reveals the names and
circumstances of Siegmund and Sieglinde, but hands over

the pieces of the broken sword, Nothung. Highly excited at this, Siegfried bids the dwarf mend the weapon, and joyously proclaims his resolve to go forth free into the world. Meanwhile he rushes out to calm the turmoil of his feelings, and Mime, whose art cannot touch the charmed steel, sinks down in despair at the prospect, of Siegfried's escape. Here Wotan enters, disguised as a wanderer, and, in a long dialogue, the two test each other's knowledge of the circumstances in which they are both interested. But when Mime is asked who will repair the sword he cannot answer. "Only he," continues Wotan, departing, "who has never known fear." Siegfried, having returned and asked in vain for the mended sword, Mime speaks to him of fear. But the young hero naïvely observes, "Is it an art? It ought to be known. So talk and tell me about it." Mime then tells him of the horrible dragon Fafner, but Siegfried merely demands to go and fight him: "Fetch me the sword, for Fear I will find." Alas, Mime cannot repair it. "Bring me the bits, then," exclaims the hero, and at once he proceeds to file them, melt the dust, and refashion the weapon. As he does so, Mime, chuckling at his own cunning, hits upon a plan to secure the fruit of Siegfried's prowess for himself, and brews a broth which shall send the victor to sleep. Joyously Siegfried works and sings till the sword is completed, and the anvil severed with it at a blow. Now

the hero feels all the might within him, and, holding the
brand aloft, he exclaims, as the curtain falls, —

> "Dead lay'st thou
> and done with long,
> now fierce like a flame is thy flash.
> Break upon wretches,
> broaden thy blaze!
> Fall on the false,
> and fell the rogue."

The second act shows us the cave in the forest
where the dragon sleeps upon the ring and hoard.
It is night, and in the darkness hither come three
schemers for the prize.   First Alberich enters, and
next Wotan, who, in the course of an altercation, is
warned by the dwarf that the ring once liberated would
work his ruin.   But Wotan trusts in his spear, the emblem
and source of his power, and, as a retort, informs Alberich
that Mime is approaching with a young hero in the hope
of gaining the ring for himself.   He even rouses the
dragon to warn him of the fate in store, and permits
Alberich to ask for the ring on condition of preventing the
combat.   But the heedless beast merely roars and goes to
sleep again.   Wotan having departed, while Alberich
conceals himself, Mime and Siegfried enter, the latter
coolly looking into the cavern without a sign of fear, and
then bidding the dwarf retire.   Left alone, Siegfried
muses about his parents, and, never having seen a
woman, tries to conjure up a picture of his mother.

Day breaks, the forest noises increase, and the birds sing in the trees. He wonders what a warbler above him means: "He says something to me ; maybe he has seen my mother." Moved by the thought, he makes a pipe with a reed, and imitates the bird in hope of learning the language. But the effort is vain, and to console himself he blows a tune on his little silver horn. This arouses Fafner, who wallows out of the hole, to be received with laughter. Mutual threats soon end in battle, and Siegfried drives Nothung into the brute's heart. Drawing back the weapon, some of the dragon's blood touches and burns his finger, which he instinctively sucks to assuage the pain. At once he knows the language of the birds, and hears them tell him to seize the ring and helm as means of power. This he proceeds to do, the two brother dwarfs entering while he is in the cavern, and having a very lively quarrel as to their respective claims on the booty. Both hide themselves as Siegfried reappears, but Mime soon proceeds to try his cunning, not, however, till after the friendly bird has told the hero that the power of the dragon's blood will enable him to hear from the dwarf's mouth what he means at heart. All Mime's intentions are thus revealed by the schemer himself, and Siegfried strikes him dead at a blow. It is now midday. Siegfried, weary, rests beneath a tree, musing on his loneliness. Nature is strong within him, and he calls on the bird to

win him the comrade he wants. For answer the bird tells
how Brünnhilde lies on her fire-guarded rock, waiting for
the man who shall claim her. The instinct of love blazes
up at this, and the curtain falls as Siegfried exultingly
follows his feathered friend along the way to the sleeping
maid. The third act opens in a wild country, amid thunder
and lightning, through which the restless and anxious
Wotan has come to consult Erda about the fate in store
for him. At the close of their interview the god rises
above considerations of self, and proclaims that the old
order shall pass away, but that the Nibelungs, or powers
of evil, shall not flourish, for Siegfried holds the ring, and
Brünnhilde shall one day redeem the world from its curse.
Erda sinks, and Siegfried enters, following his bird. Now,
for the first time, he encounters Wotan, and shows him so
little respect that the god, becoming angry, bars the way
with his spear. Once had Nothung touched that divine
weapon, and had shivered to pieces; but now it is the
spear that breaks, and with it the power of the gods.
Exclaiming, "Go on; my hand cannot hold thee!"
Wotan vanishes from the scene to prepare for the doom
that awaits him. On him, also, and his order has the
curse fallen. Brünnhilde's guarding fire is now reflected
from the mountain tops, and presently fills the stage with
smoke and flame, through which, blowing his horn,
Siegfried plunges. On the clouds of vapour rising we

behold once more the sleeping Brünnhilde, covered with her armour, while Siegfried from the height of a rock surveys her with wonder. Approaching, he removes the shield, takes off the helmet, and is astonished at the "clustering clouds" of hair, which "border in billows a laughing lake of heaven." Next, he tries to undo the breast-plate, but can only succeed by severing the iron rings with his sword. At once the Woman is revealed, and *for the first time the strong Man knows fear.* Siegfried is lost in amazement. "What have I come to ! Can I be a coward ? " he exclaims, as he kneels to waken Brünnhilde with a kiss. Slowly the maid lifts herself, hails the sun, and asks who is the hero of her resurrection. She recognises Siegfried, and tells him, with rapture, how she had striven to carry out the directions of Wotan, and had suffered for the deed. None of this Siegfried understands. To him Brünnhilde is merely the woman, and as such he impetuously approaches her. But the divinity is still existent, and the maid holds him aloof in, wonder and alarm, entreating him to leave her. Presently a change takes place. Human instincts awaken, and hero and heroine passionately embrace, with words that express the highest rapture of love. At this point the curtain falls, and another resting-place in the course of the drama is reached.

It is hard to resist here the inducements which tempt

me to dwell upon the drama I have outlined, and to discuss, if only for one's own satisfaction, its combined ingenuity and beauty. But the poem of *Der Ring des Nibelungen* should be considered as a whole, and I pass on to the general effect made by the representation. As may be imagined from the nature of the subject and the sternness with which Wagner carries out his theory that the situation and sentiment should dictate the music, there is much in the first act not beautiful. Wonderfully clever as a piece of musical mosaic, and fertile in resource of expression as it may be, no pleasure is given to the listener who cannot find all his interest excited by the verses and incidents with which it is connected. An exception must be made, however, in favour of the music serving to express the abounding life of Siegfried. Than this nothing could be happier. The orchestra overflows with vigour, and works up a striking *motif*—not unlike that of Handel's "Let us break their bonds asunder "—with masterful power. Still more obviously must all the music of the sword-welding scene be excepted. Here again the effect is one of overwhelming force. The young giant at the forge sings in the exuberance of his life and strength, and the orchestra is gigantic also, rolling out a torrent of sound which sweeps before it all doubt and cavil. But the second act is the gem of the work, as those who recall the poetic feeling

which dominates it will be prepared to hear. Over the
meeting of Alberich and Wotan we may pass (though
every page of the score is a marvel of ingenuity) to
arrive at the point where Siegfried enters. Here the
characteristic tendency of Wagner as a Gothic artist *pur
sang* brings the grotesque and the beautiful face to face.
What more grotesque than the dragon's shapeless bulk,
swinging tail, and roaring voice? On the other hand, what
more beautiful than the idea of the birds filling the forest
with their warblings and talking to the hero in language
which he, by marvellous means, has learned to understand?
Happily, too, the beautiful predominates, for Wagner, in
poem and music, has dwelt upon the situation lovingly.
His orchestral picturing is wonderful in its clearness and
fascinating in its charm. We hear the forest sounds
almost as though a forest itself were audible. The low
hum of life falls upon the ear, birds twitter in the
branches, and the entire scene is perfectly idyllic in its
sweet naturalness. It lasts long, but not too long,
and, though interrupted by a combat of man and brute
such as no stage art can make other than absurd, we look
back upon it at the close as upon that which has moved
imagination and sense to a height of pleasure rarely
attained. Here too, as always when the verses suggest
it, the vocal phrases, disjointed though they be, have
melodic charm. But the effect should be taken as a

whole, and so regarded the Siegfried portion of this act is recognised as a masterpiece of compound art—a grand addition to the world's store of beauty. In the third act the music to the interview of Wotan and Erda contains some impressive passages, and more than ever excites admiration of the skill with which Wagner interweaves the large number of *motifs* he has now accumulated. But the interest grows when Siegfried is brought face to face with Brünnhilde, and a dialogue begins destined to end with a love duet unexampled in its stress of passion. Comparisons are here invited between this scene and that in the first act of *Die Walküre*, which I cannot but look upon as in some respects superior. Nevertheless, whether regarded for itself or by comparison, the Siegfried and Brünnhilde duet is a striking example of intense musical expression. As regards the relative merits of *Die Walküre* and *Siegfried*, the general opinion is in favour of the first, on account of more absolute beauty, springing from poetic suggestiveness and strong human interest. All the same, however, will *Siegfried* stand among Wagnerian dramas as a stupendous work. So it was regarded last night, and after each act shouts of applause filled the theatre.

The cast of *Siegfried* was as follows: Siegfried, Georg Unger; Mime, Carl Schlosser; Der Wanderer, Franz Betz; Alberich, Carl Hill; Fafner, Franz von Reichenberg; Erda, Luise Jäde; Brünnhilde, Amalie Materna. Of these artists only the representative of the title-character appeared for the first time, the others having had work to do in *Das Rheingold* or *Die Walküre*. Herr Unger, who is a Bayreuth man, was specially chosen by Wagner to represent his favourite hero, and justifies the choice alike on account of his personal appearance, dramatic ability, and powerful voice. Tall and stately, conveying an impression of great physical strength, and able to identify himself thoroughly with the character, he made as good a Siegfried as we had any right to expect. Unfortunately, like not a few of his colleagues, Herr Unger cannot sing, and when a true vocal phrase falls to his lot he simply abuses it. But he can declaim with immense vigour, which is a qualification for Wagner's music-drama not to be despised. Among others who distinguished themselves in *Siegfried* were Herr Schlosser, an extraordinarily perfect Mime, and Frau Materna, who, in the scene of Brünnhilde's waking, sustained her part like the accomplished artist she is. This lady's vocal skill would appear to better advantage in opera, but the quality and power of her tones, as well as the impressiveness of her acting, could have had no finer demonstration. For the rest, it will be enough to say that all worked together with a smoothness and attention to detail which threw fresh light upon the possibilities of the lyric stage. Every artist knew what to do and did it, not only as though individuality had been sunk

F

in the character, but as though success depended upon each one alone. I have so often and so warmly praised the orchestra that nothing new remains for me to say. But the theme is one of which I could never tire, so much does every fresh hearing impress upon me a sense of perfection. There were times during the performance of *Siegfried* when the orchestra was left alone to carry on the idea of the drama, and on every such occasion—for which, by-the-way, Wagner seems to have reserved some of his happiest thoughts—the musical impression deepened to profundity. Such purity of tone, perfect oneness of expression, and everchanging glory of colour amounted to a revelation of before unimagined artistic beauty. The scenic effects and stage management generally were again all that could be desired, especially fine being the break of day in the forest, and the representation of the fire through which Siegfried passes to Brünnhilde. Some doubt was felt about the dragon and the bird, such stage creatures being always liable to make themselves ridiculous; but no mishap chanced, and Mr. Dykwynkyn may congratulate himself on an important contribution to the success of *Der Ring des Nibelungen.*

BAYREUTH, AUG. 18.

I COME now to the *Götterdämmerung*, or "Dusk of the Gods," which, like its immediate predecessor, had never before been heard in public. About the curiosity excited, the eager gathering at the theatre, and the zest with which everybody settled down when the trumpets heralded the rising of the curtain, it is unnecessary again to speak. Enough that the first notes broke in upon an absolute silence, which, as far as the audience were concerned, reigned during the hour and three-quarters occupied by the prologue and first act. Continuing the course of the "argument," let me remind the reader that at the close of *Siegfried* the ring and tarn-helm remained with the hero, who, however, in the simpleness of his "pure humanity," knew nothing definite about their power. Since then he has learned much wisdom from the lips of Brünnhilde, with whom he dwells, and from whom he is about to part in quest of adventure. The curtain rises on Brünnhilde's rock while it is yet night, and reveals the three Norns, or Fates, representatives of the Past, Present, and Future, discoursing upon the events which, by bringing about the downfall of the gods, will change the order of the world. From them we learn that Wotan has surrounded Walhalla with the wood of the world-ash out of which he cut the shaft of his now broken spear, and that he and all his heroes solemnly await their doom. On the disappearance of the Fates, day breaks gloriously, and Siegfried enters, accompanied by Brünnhilde, who has given him her horse Grane and clothed him with her own discarded armour. In return Siegfried bestows upon her the fatal ring, and, after an impassioned farewell, rides away, Brünnhilde watching till the sound of his horn fades in distance. With this the prologue ends. The curtain again rising, we are transported to the Hall of King Gunther, on the Rhine, and see the King, his sister Gutrune, and half-brother Hagen sitting at a table commanding a view of the beautiful river. The first two have no connection with any previous event or character in the drama, but it is otherwise with Hagen. Like Wotan, Alberich had resolved to train up a hero of his own race who should fight for the ring; and Hagen is the son upon whom his hopes rest. We now see this fresh schemer for the accursed bauble begin his work by stimulating in Gunther a passion for Brünnhilde, and vaunting to Gutrune the glorious person and achievements of Siegfried. His plan contemplates the love of Siegfried for Gutrune, which is only to be gratified by his winning Brünnhilde for Gunther. All are ignorant of Siegfried's relations with Brünnhilde: but lest his affections should be engaged Hagen will brew him a drink certain to cause forgetfulness of her who holds his heart. The scheme is approved; and Siegfried, who opportunely appears, receives a warm invitation to remain as a guest. He does so, takes the welcome-cup—Hagen's charmed draught—from Gutrune's hands, and at once, forgetting Brünnhilde, falls in love with her. Pursuing his advantage, Gunther declares his passion for Brünnhilde, and receives from Siegfried a prompt offer of his services—"Me frights not her fire; I'll woo for thee the maid." In return Gunther promises that Gutrune shall be his wife, and the two swear blood-brotherhood to clench the bargain, the scene closing as they set out for Brünnhilde's abode, advised by Hagen of the power of the tarn-helm hanging from Siegfried's belt. The rock is now once more shown, just as comes storming through the sky Waltraute, one of the Walkyries. Her mission to Brünnhilde is a serious one, and grand and gloomy is the picture she draws of Wotan sitting silent in his doomed castle.

> " So sits he,
> and breathes not a sound.
> on stately stool
> uncheered and still,
> the splintered weapon
> fixed in his span."

Only once he had spoken, and then, in a dream, whispered,—

> " The day the River's Daughters
> find from her finger the ring,
> will the curse's weight
> be cast from god and the world."

Hearing this, Waltraute slipped "through the ranges of

wordless warmen," mounted her horse, and rode to Brünnhilde. We now hear her entreat that the ring might be
surrendered to the Rhine Daughters. But Brünnhilde,
with the sublime selfishness of love, sees in it only
Siegfried's gift, and exclaims,—

> " More than Walhall's welfare,
> more than the good of the gods,
> the ring I guard."

In despair, Waltraute rides away, the encircling fire, as
she does so, blazing up, and Siegfried's horn sounding a
merry note in the distance. Brünnhilde runs to greet her
hero, and sees him indeed, but in the form of Gunther, a
change which the tarn-helm had made possible. What
follows may be imagined. In the utmost terror and
distress, Brünnhilde reproaches the absent Wotan for
bringing her to such "shame and darkness." But her
suffering has no effect upon Siegfried, who exclaims,—

> " The night is near ;
> and rest in thy room
> halves by his right thy husband."

Solemnly, then, Brünnhilde points to the pledge of
Siegfried's love, only to have it taken away forcefully
by the pretended Gunther. With the loss of the ring
Brünnhilde's resolution seems to depart, and, at the
bidding of the intruder, she leads the way to her resting-
place. Siegfried follows, but as he does so draws his
sword, with the words,—

" Now, Nothung, witness well
that faithfully I wooed ;
lest I wane in truth to my brother,
bar me away from his bride."

This closes the first act. When next the curtain rises
we are again at Gunther's Hall. It is night, and
Hagen watches, armed with shield and spear. But
he is not alone. His father Alberich has come up
from the Nibelung's gloomy abode to stimulate his
zeal for the ring, and now receives an assurance that
all shall be attempted for its recovery. Day breaks, and
the mists clear away, showing the Rhine in its beauty.
At this point Siegfried enters in his own proper person,
having escorted Brünnhilde to the spot where Gunther
awaited her, and then, by the tarn-helm's power, trans-
ferred himself hither. Informed that the King approaches
with the bride whom another has won, Hagen summons
the warriors of Gunther, who answer the call, and, at his
bidding, prepare a suitable reception. The strangely mated
pair now arrive, greeted by a chorus of welcome; the
King triumphant, Brünnhilde cast down, despairing, and
speechless. But when the still unconscious Siegfried
advances to meet her, leading Gutrune, she finds both
voice and vigour; amazement changing to fiercest anger
as she sees upon Siegfried's finger the deadly ring he, in
changing places after the winning of Brünnhilde, had
omitted to bestow upon Gunther. The whole trick then

stands revealed, and love turns to desire for vengeance.
"Gods of my heaven," exclaims Brünnhilde, "find me a
vengeance unvaunted before! Rouse me to rage never
wreaked on a wrong." The means of retribution are at
once obvious, and Brünnhilde asserts in the hearing of all
that which is understood as a declaration of Siegfried's
faithlessness to his trust for Gunther. Boldly the hero
avows his innocence, exclaiming,—

> "Nothung, my shameless sword,
> sheltered the truth I swore."

Unhesitatingly, moreover, he makes oath to a like effect
upon Hagen's spear :—

> "Where a death can stab me,
> strike me dead;
> wrought I what rights her blame,
> failed I my brother in faith!"

In turn, Brünnhilde makes oath to the contrary, and
the situation grows critical till Siegfried closes it by
saying that "women's grudge soon is outgrown," and
bidding all prepare the feast. The stage is now left to
Gunther, who flings himself down in an agony of shame,
Brünnhilde, who stands gloomily apart, and Hagen, who,
having work to do, sets about it by offering himself as a
champion to redress the injured woman's wrong. So does
he excite the feelings of both that Brünnhilde informs
Hagen where Siegfried is vulnerable to the point of his
spear, and Gunther, despite the vow of blood-brotherhood,

agrees to a plan for his death. The act ends as the bridal procession of Siegfried and Gutrune crosses the stage. When the curtain rises for the last time, we look on a picturesque valley opening to the shore of the Rhine, and see the three river-nymphs gambolling in the water as they await the hero who possesses their lost treasure. Siegfried, having wandered from his companions in pursuit of a bear, appears, and is entreated by the Rhine Daughters to give up the ring, which, however, he refuses to do. With mocking words the nymphs vanish, to be called back by Siegfried, who, annoyed at their taunts, is willing to part with the bauble. But they will not now accept it, saying,—

> "Withhold it, hero,
> and ward it well,
> until thou hast read the hurt
> thou harbourest in the ring."

" Now, sing what you foresee," answers Siegfried. In response the Rhine Daughters tell him about the curse of which he himself will that day be a victim. But to no avail. Siegfried laughs at fear, declaring that were the ring worth nothing he would not buy safety with it. Upon this the maidens leave him, and Siegfried reflects that women on land and women in water are very much alike: "whom flattery fails to thaw, with threats they think to fright him." The hunting party, including Gunther and Hagen, now enter the glen, and as

they refresh themselves, Siegfried lightly speaks of the
nymphs and their prophecy, rallies the King on his settled
sadness, and offers to tell a story of his youth. All
gather round as Siegfried narrates the adventure with the
dragon up to the point at which the bird led him on to
Brünnhilde. Here he would have stopped for lack of
memory had not the crafty Hagen given him another
drink which released the spell of the first. Thus enabled
to go on, he speaks of the fire-guarded maiden and how
he won her, to the horror and shame of the listening
King. Now has come the time for vengeance. Diverting
Siegfried's attention, Hagen spears him, and the hero
dies with words of love for Brünnhilde upon his lips.
Sadly the warriors bear his body homewards, where, by
a change of scene, we arrive as Hagen enters calling
for torches to welcome "the quarry from the hunt."
The mournful crowd approach, and Gutrune throws
herself on Siegfried's body, wildly accusing her brother
of his murder. But Gunther points to Hagen; nor
does the Nibelung's son shrink from avowing alike his
crime and purpose :—

> " Meetly I've wrought and made
> boundless my right of booty ;
> which so I seize in this ring."

Gunther intervenes, and after a short struggle is killed.
"Now," again exclaims Hagen, "the ring!" He grasps

at the treasure, but all fall back in horror as the hand of the corpse closes and raises itself threateningly. At that moment Brünnhilde appears, advances to the body, aud sadly looks down upon it. After a long silence she bids the men prepare a funeral pile on the river's bank, calls for her horse Grane, and takes the ring from the dead man's finger. She has made a high resolve. As a supreme act of love she will sacrifice herself in the flames which consume the body of Siegfried—flames which will redeem the world from the curse of the ring by melting it and restoring to the river its gold. Making a passionate address to her horse, she plunges with him into the fire, the river at that moment rising and advancing, bearing the Rhine Daughters aloft on its waves. "Back from the ring," exclaims Hagen, darting into the flood, only to be dragged beneath its waters by two of the nymphs, while the third holds up exultingly the recovered treasure. As the curtain slowly falls we see afar in the northern sky the flames of the burning Walhalla, and watch the gods silently encounter their doom. The old order has passed away; the warlike deities are no more, and love rules the world.

It must be obvious that in this closing part of the great drama we are confronted by circumstances varying iu most important respects from those before met with. The story of the *Götterdämmerung* is one which Verdi might have set to music, so rapidly do the situations follow each other, so intense is their dramatic interest, and so great are the opportunities for the effects which modern opera loves. By comparison, the earlier sections of *Der Ring des Nibelungen* are merely dialogues with an orchestral accompaniment; whereas here we have a libretto closely approaching the generally accepted model. This being so, the result of its combination with Wagner's system—above all in the matter of the concerted music—is curious to note. I cannot see how Wagner here escapes the charge of inconsistency. Had he, in his striving after realism, asserted that people do not speak the same words at the same time, and acted up to the fact by rigidly excluding concerted vocal pieces, his position would have been logical. But he admits such things. He does so in *Das Rheingold*, again in *Die Walküre*, and again in the *Götterdämmerung*, where, for example, Gunther's men answer Hagen's summons in chorus. Yet, again and again, when—the theory of a chorus being admitted—concerted music is called for, nothing of the kind appears. If the warriors may acclaim Gunther and Brünnhilde, why are they silent when Hagen kills Siegfried? Why no exclamations as the hero's body is received by the King's household? Above all, why is the stage filled with a crowd of dummies during the magnificent and moving last scene? The absence of a chorus here is the very wantonness of whim. It excites an

annoying sense of incompleteness, and makes us cry even
beneath the roof of Wagner's theatre, "Oh for a Verdi!"
But had the master employed ever so freely the splendid
resources that lay ready to his hand it is doubtful whether
the dramatic power of *Götterdämmerung* would not have
put the music in a secondary place. Whatever may be
said of other sections of the work, here the story and the
poetry well-nigh absorb attention. To this rule, however,
there are exceptions. The conference of the Norns in the
prologue would be simply unendurable but for the cease-
less stream of music from the orchestra; and the same
may be said of a few other passages. But as a whole the
drama fascinates us, and that most where most appears to
be wanting in its musical treatment. This is fortunate,
because a good deal is wanting—so much that I have no
hesitation in giving the *Götterdämmerung* the third place
in regard to music, ranking it after *Die Walküre* and
Siegfried, Das Rheingold coming last of all. The result
may be in a measure due to the fact that it presents little
of novelty. According to a very careful analysis by Herr
von Wolzogen there are in *Der Ring des Nibelungen* ninety
distinct *motivi*, of which thirty-five belong to *Das Rheingold*,
twenty-two to *Die Walküre*, twenty to *Siegfried*, and only
thirteen to *Götterdämmerung*, which thus has, with small
relief, to bear the burden of constantly repeating themes
already heard over and over again. But apart from this

it may be said, speaking very generally, that the music presents fewer than usual of those passages which are remembered chiefly for their own sake. The listeners to the *Götterdämmerung* go away impressed, but if asked to recall what they have heard they find that memory is busy only with the drama, and that of the music it retains an impression definite only with regard to features which produced weariness. As a music-drama therefore—I speak, of course, with the reserve due to the limited acquaintance of a single hearing—the *Götterdämmerung* disappoints, the more keenly because of the magnificent opportunities supplied by its situations for really sublime musical effect.

I can touch but lightly on the performance. Frau Materna, as Brünnhilde, exerted herself unsparingly, and won a triumph of the highest rank. In the last act she met stern requirements in a manner possible only to a great artist. Wagner owes her much, for another Brünnhilde, her equal, would be hard to find. Herr Unger was again Siegfried, and Herr Hill, Alberich; the characters introduced for the first time being thus distributed: Gunther, Eugen Gura; Gutrune, Mathilde Weckerlin; Hagen, Gustav Siehr. Of the chorus I cannot speak too highly, while of the orchestra, the matchless orchestra, it is impossible to say more than that it was worthy of itself. From beginning to end the stage-effects were splendid. Few will forget the daybreak after the Norns had disappeared, or that which revealed the Rhine. Fewer still can cease to recall the effect of Siegfried's funeral pyre as the flames gained hold on Gunther's palace and the beams came crashing down, while the whole sky was made red by the burning Walhalla. Nothing more terribly real was ever put upon the stage, and with it appropriately closed a series of representations unequalled for scenic truth and grandeur.

CONCLUSIONS.

SEPT. 21.

WEEKS have passed since the final performance of *Der Ring des Nibelungen;* the artists and amateurs whom the genius and will of a single man summoned to Bayreuth from all parts of the world have gone home; the doors of the Festival Theatre are shut and the keys put away; distance of time has done much to dissipate the glamour of notable doings, and now, far better than at any earlier moment, is it possible to arrive at just conclusions respecting Richard Wagner's "new art." But before entering upon this task, let me repudiate any sympathy with those—must I style them critics?—who seem to have visited Bayreuth for no higher purpose than sneer and sarcasm. One might have thought that such, in Wagner's case, antiquated and ineffective weapons would not again be forthcoming, if only as the result of their obvious worthlessness. Wagner has been the butt of ridicule for more than twenty years, and the answer to all is—Bayreuth. Yet many of his opponents continue to fight on in the old fashion. No wonder that "the Master" is serenely disdainful. No wonder, either, that people who care little about the questions at issue begin to be impatient, and to ask whether the cheap argument of a sneer, and the loose, if lively, logic of a joke exhaust the arsenal of his enemies. Depend upon it that neither Wagner himself nor Wagnerian theories are to be put down by such means. The man is probably unconquerable anyhow; and his theories, so gravely and powerfully advanced, so unreservedly accepted by thousands whose judgment commands respect, and so important that their formal illustration occupies the mind of the civilised world, are at least entitled to serious treatment. This I now propose to give them, animated less by a desire to find matter for rejection than to discover that which may be accepted as an addition to the resources of art.

The subject of Wagner's new music-drama presents itself in two grand divisions—first, the poem; secondly, the music—and so intimate is the connection between these that the study of one must be carried on in view of and largely in the light of the other. That they are separable is true; but a discussion of the poem of *Der Ring des Nibelungen* as a poem, or of the music without reference to its application, would have small practical value. It is not my business, therefore, to estimate Wagner as a poet merely, or as a composer merely, but as the creator of a form of art in which the outcome of both capacities appears

G

under novel conditions. This does not prevent reference to certain facts lying, so to speak, outside of argument. And first, as regards the sources whence Wagner drew the materials for his great drama, it may be well to state that he has largely used the liberty which constitutes one of the advantages of the myth. In dealing with purely traditional, as distinct from historic themes, the dramatist is absolutely unfettered, and in *Der Ring des Nibelungen* Wagner avails himself alike of Teutonic, Scandinavian, and Icelandic sources for incident, character, and situation, taking "here a little and there a little," as seemed good to him. A German critic, who ought to have known better, has assailed the poem on this very account, taunting Wagner with putting forward as a representative national art-work that which is but in small part made up of German materials. But surely, having to deal with a myth belonging in varied shapes to a group of peoples sprung from the same stock, Wagner was justified in acting as though all its forms were a common inheritance. The German has, as a matter of family privilege, scarcely less right to the legends of Scandinavia or Iceland than the inhabitants of those countries themselves—to say nothing of the fact that in this instance the chief scenes of the story are laid on the banks of the Rhine. As regards the particular subject chosen, it should be remembered that the whole drama of *Der Ring des Nibelungen*

grew up around the person of the hero Siegfried, by whom
the master was first attracted. To a mind so full of
romanticism, and so accustomed, as in *Der Fliegende
Holländer*, *Tannhäuser*, and *Lohengrin*, to deal with
legendary material, the person, character, and achievements of Siegfried were irresistible. The *Völsunga Saga*,
as translated by Messrs. Magnusson and Morris, says of
this mighty man of old,—

" He was far above other men in courtesy and goodly manners, and
well-nigh in all things else ; and when as folk tell of all the mightiest
champions and the noblest chiefs, then ever is he named the foremost,
and his name goes wide about on all tongues north of the sea of the
Greek lands, and even so shall it be while the world endures. Now
the hair of this Sigurd (Siegfried) was golden-red of hue, fair of fashion,
and falling down in great locks ; thick and short was his beard, and of
no other colour ; high-nosed he was, broad and high-boned of face ;
so keen were his eyes that few durst gaze up under the brows of him ;
his shoulders were as broad to look on as the shoulders of two. . . .
Wise he was to know things yet undone ; and the voice of all fowls he
knew, wherefore few things fell on him unawares. Of many words
he was, and so fair of speech withal that, whensoever he made it his
business to speak, he never left speaking before that to all men it
seemed full sure that no otherwise must the matter be than as he
said. . . . Never did he lose heart, and of nought was he adrad."

From such a hero as this it was not likely that Wagner
would turn away, or that, as the charm of the theme grew
upon him, he would resist the temptation to enlarge the
scope of his labours, taking in all that led up to or was in
any way essentially connected with the central figure.
With what success he performed his task, and in what

consequent degree the poem bears out the excellence of Wagner's theories, are matters of opinion, and belong to the general subject for discussion.

About the admissibility of legend for dramatic purposes, recognised as it has been from the earliest times by all nations, there can arise no question. But few will agree with Wagner that legend is the dramatist's only true resource. In an elaborate argument—" Opera and Drama "—he has attacked both the historical and domestic romance as a groundwork for stage plays— proving, to his own satisfaction at least, that the first, with its endless ramifications and cumbersome accessories, is unfit for the modern theatre, which insists upon a *realisation* of scene, and will not be content, as in Shakespeare's day, with its *intimation* only. He pictures the modern poet as standing " inquiringly and confused " before the realised historico-romantic play, and says, " The Shakespearian drama had produced upon him, in a literary point of view, the elevating impression of the most perfect poetical unity, as long as it had merely appealed to his imagination, which was capable of culling from it an harmonious and well-defined picture. But the poet now beheld that picture fade completely from before his eyes in the fulfilment of the wish to see it realised to the senses." This, according to Wagner, had a twofold result. It com- pelled the poet, as in the case of Goethe's *Faust*, to write

" literary dramas for silent perusal," ignoring the stage altogether, or it drove him back, for a practical representation of his conceptions, upon the forms of antiquity, as in *Iphigenia in Aulis*. But when adopting the second course he was compelled, as Wagner carefully points out, to choose the subject from the mythos, with which alone it was possible to attain the desired end. It must be confessed that the master's position here is hard to assail, because his indictment against the historic romance as a groundwork for drama finds powerful support in the illustrious authors who using it have at the same time ignored the stage, and in the conspicuous failures where actual representation has been intended. Passing on to the domestic romance, as we have it in *Fidelio*, or, as connected with historical adjuncts and raised to its highest pitch of importance, in *Egmont*, Wagner admits one advantage viz. " the possibility of scenic representation, because in no instance do necessities for the *mise-en-scène* arise out of the scanty action which the *mise-en-scène* is not fundamentally able to satisfy." But he brings against it a charge which had better be stated in his own words for the consideration of those who, predisposed to accept his opinions because they are his, would give up Fidelios and Egmonts for Tannhäusers and Lohengrins. Here is the charge in question : " The characteristic element of the romance of domestic life consists in the

fact that the action on which it is founded is perfectly
separated from the more comprehensive connection of
historical events and. relations, retains only the social
precipitate of these historical events as conditional
adjuncts—which, in reality, are only the reaction of
the said historical occurrences deadened so as to become
colourless—and developes itself more according to moods
imperatively enjoined by these adjuncts than according to
inward motives capable of perfect plastic utterance. This
action is just as limited and poor as the moods of mind
by which it is called forth are devoid of freedom and
" independent inwardness." The ultimate reference of all
argument on matters affecting human consciousness is
to that consciousness itself, and those of us who have
not yet discovered that the romance of domestic life is
made up of the social precipitate of historic events,
deadened and colourless, or that both its action and
causative moods of mind are limited and poor, may rest
satisfied that we are not in error while the universal heart
finds here that to which it can respond, that which excites
the noblest emotions and aspirations. Referring to the
origin of myth, Wagner says, "Art is, according to its
purport, nothing more than the fulfilment of the wish
to recognise oneself again in the phenomena of the
outward world. The artist says to himself in the object
he has represented, 'Thus art thou, thus dost thou feel

and think, and thus wouldst thou act if thou couldst act according to the choice of thy wish.'" Precisely, and the modern man sees in the drama of domestic romance that which he is, or may be, with infinitely more clearness than he can recognise himself in the heroes of mythic lore. Wherefore to him the domestic drama more apparently fulfils the purpose of art.

Passing on to Wagner's direct advocacy of the myth, and premising that he cannot here be followed through the arguments adduced, three propositions are met with. First, the myth is a poem, "produced by a general way of looking at life;" that is to say, it arises from the impulse of the people to give an intelligible representation of natural phenomena which otherwise perplexes and is a cause of anxiety. Secondly, tragedy is "nothing more than the artistic perfection of the myth." Thirdly, the tragic poet "simply communicates the purport and nature of the myth in the most convincing and intelligible manner." Few will care, perhaps, to dispute these theses; the less because the main fact that the myth presents valuable material for dramatic purposes is beyond question. There are, however, myths and myths; some big with human interest even under modern conditions of life—with which alone can it be supposed that "the people" are acquainted—others located far off, surrounded by a cold and unsympathetic atmosphere. In the second class must indubitably be placed those which are concerned less with man than with supernatural creations. That this is not Wagner's opinion, however, his *Ring des Nibelungen* proves, and he would probably defend the position he has taken up by a reference to his favourite models, the dramatists of Greece. But the conditions under which the Greek masters wrote were different from those obtaining now—so different that it is barely possible for us to estimate their significance. "Religion to a Greek," says a contemporary author, "consisted in an intense love of all that is beautiful, and a firm belief that every stream and tree and cloud was tenanted by a god. All that for us is mere senseless imagery was for him a reality. In the sound of a stream he really believed that he heard the sighing or the laughter of a nymph—how should the stream move and speak if it were not so possessed ? The clouds gathered and the lightning flashed, not of themselves, or in obedience to laws of nature—of those mysterious powers the Greek had never heard—but simply because some person moved the clouds and hurled the lightning ; and this was Zeus or Jove." When, therefore, Æschylus placed upon the Athenian stage his *Prometheus Bound,* or the wonderful trilogy which unfolds the story of Orestes, he kept strictly within the perception, consciousness, and sympathy of his public. Zeus, Strength, Force, Vulcan, Oceanus, Io, " the maid by gadfly driven," Apollo, and the

Furies, were all real to the Athenians ; but what are they, and such as they, to us ? Mere abstractions, incapable of being more than intellectually perceived; shadows that the mind's eye can discern, but which touch us nowhere. Moreover, it is to be observed that even the Greek drama-tists, obeying an instinct as well as consciously meeting an artistic necessity, were careful to secure a strong human interest. If they set forth the action of the gods, it was action having man as its object, and not, as in *Der Ring des Nibelungen*, the conservation of godlike power. Take the trilogy already cited. No personage was ever more real to an Athenian audience than Agamemnon, and, start-ing from this point of close contact, the whole story, through the vengeance of Orestes and his punishment, to the installation of the Eumenides as guardians of Athens, was a powerful appeal to the sympathy of those for whom Æschylus wrote. It is vain, therefore, for Wagner to set up a pretended parallelism between the Greek drama and that which, taking *Der Ring des Nibelungen* as a sample, he would establish in this nineteenth century after Christ. The old pagan myth is as dead as the dodo in so far as regards its power over the popular mind. Yet Wagner has not only declined to recognise this fact, but acted as though the very reverse were the case. Upon what, for instance, does the drama of *Der Ring des Nibelungen* turn? Upon a struggle for supremacy, represented by a talisman, between supernatural beings, in the course of which man is introduced merely as an agent, Wotan (Odin) on the one hand, and Alberich on the other, allying themselves with humanity in order to produce each a champion whose personal encounter brings the drama to its crisis.   In the whole work there are thirty-four characters, of whom only seven are mortal, and of these seven only three—Gutrune, Gunther, and Hunding—are pure mortals, the others— Sieglinde, Siegmund, Siegfried, and Hagen—being the descendants of Wotan or Alberich.   Later on I shall have occasion to show that this preponderance of the supernatural element arose from no necessity of the subject, but from Wagner's deliberate choice; for the present I desire only to ask how it is possible that a work so constructed can commend itself as the model drama of the future.   We barely realise Wotan, Alberich, Fafner, and the rest of the contending agents at all; and as to the issue, if, as Milton said, the battles of the Saxon Heptarchy are of no more interest now than so many skirmishes of kites and crows, how much can we care who gains the fateful ring ?

The task of showing that the preponderance of the supernatural in *Der Ring des Nibelungen* is not a heavy one, inasmuch as in the Icelandic " Story of the Volsungs and Niblungs " the chief events of Wagner's drama are found almost entirely separated from the gods and goddesses of Walhalla.   Odin (Wotan) appears now and then, it is true, and it is impossible not to admire the superior art of his introduction as compared with that shown in *Der Ring des Nibelungen*. Wagner makes such large use of this chief of the Northern deities, and places him in such positions, that, quite apart from his terribly long-winded utterances, we soon begin to regard him with contempt, and resent his presence as that of a bore. On the other hand, the legend shows him rapidly flitting across the stage in mysterious guise, bent on purposes at which the myth-maker never ventures to guess. Here is the description of his appearing at the wedding of Signy (Sieglinde) and King Siggeir (the Hunding of *Die Walküre*):—

"The tale tells that great fires were made endlong the hall, and the great tree aforesaid stood midmost thereof; withal folks say that, when as men sat by the fires in the evening, a certain man came into the hall, unknown of aspect to all men; and suchlike array he had that over him was a spotted cloak, and he was barefoot, and had linen breeches knit tight even unto the bone, and he had a sword in his hand as he went up to the Branstock, and a slouched hat upon his head; huge he was, and seeming ancient and one-eyed. So he drew his sword, and smote it into the tree-trunk, so that it sank in up to the hilt; and all held back from greeting the man. Then he took up the sword and said, 'Whoso draweth this sword from this stock shall have the same as a gift from me, and shall find in good sooth that never bare he better sword in hand than is this.' Therewith out went the old man from the hall, and none knew who he was or whither he went."

Ever when Odin enters into the story it is for such a brief moment, attended by circumstances which invest him with awe and mystery. For the rest, nearly all there is of the supernatural belongs to the tale told by Regin (Wagner's Mime) to Sigurd with reference to the treasure guarded by Fafner. Here the brother of the " Worm " is represented to be able to take the shape of an otter, while Andvari—the original Alberich—wears the form of a pike. Apart from these things the story of the Volsungs belongs to humanity, and is a record, marked by beautiful simplicity and profound pathos, of human doings. Yet, as I have said, the chief events of *Der Ring des Nibelungen* are found in it, from the gaining by Fafner of the accursed ring to Brünnhilde's self-sacrifice after Siegfried's death. Moreover, the Icelandic original preserves a decency which Wagner, resolved that the " purely human " should be indeed " free from all conventionality," has wilfully set at nought. In the legend, as in the drama, the Volsung race is perpetuated by incest, but with the important difference that Signy (Sieglinde) presents herself to her brother disguised as a " witchwife," and is not recognised. Wagner, on the other hand, makes Siegmund utter the now famous exclamation,—

> " Bride and sister be thou to thy brother ;
> so blossom the Walsung's blood."

Nor are these by any means the only points in which the Icelandic legend contrasts favourably with the drama. Many instances of true naturalness and unaffected pathos are either perverted by Wagner, or altogether overlooked, and a few of them may be cited with advantage. It will be remembered that when Brünnhilde is brought home by Gunther as his bride, she detects Siegfried's fraud by seeing on his finger the ring which he had wrested from her after riding through the fire in Gunther's form. How from that moment she becomes a fury bent upon vengeance no reader of *Götterdämmerung* needs to be told. The blunt directness of all this is the exact opposite to the poetic beauty of the Icelandic version. There we find the discovery arise from some hasty word uttered by Gutrune as she and Brünnhilde assert the superior merits of their respective husbands. "Little it beseems thee of all folk," exclaims Siegfried's wife to her sister-in-law, "to mock him who was thy first beloved. And Fafner he slew, yea, and he rode thy flaming fire, whereas thou didst deem that he was Gunnar (Gunther) the King; and by thy side he lay, and took from thine hand the ring, Andvari's loom; here mayst thou well behold it." The chronicle continues with touching simplicity: "Then Brünnhilde saw the ring, and knew it, and waxed as wan as a dead woman, and she went home and spake no word the evening long." Thenceforth to the end Brünnhilde is majestic in her anger and grief, bearing no semblance to the ranting madwoman of Wagner's play. One and another go to cheer her, but she is either silent or speaks

words like these to her husband : " Never again seest thou
me glad in thine hall, never drinking, never at the chess-
play, never speaking the words of kindness, never over-
laying the fair cloths with gold, never giving thee good
counsel. Ah ! my sorrow of heart, that I might not get
Siegfried to me !" Siegfried himself addresses her :
"Awake, Brünnhilde ! The sun shineth now over all the
house, and thou hast slept enough ; cast off grief from thee
and take up gladness." But the answer is : " This is the
sorest sorrow to me, that the bitter sword is not reddened
in thy blood." Whereto Siegfried replies, in the prophetic
spirit of those marked for death, and with most affecting
resignation, " Have no fear thereof ! No long while to
wait ere the bitter sword stand deep in my heart ; and no
worse needest thou to pray for thyself, for thou wilt not
live when I am dead. The days of our two lives shall be
few enough from henceforth." How Brünnhilde will not
be reconciled to her husband till he has avenged her on
Siegfried, how the hero is stabbed in his bed by Gunther's
young brother, who had sworn no oath of friendship, and
Brünnhilde—the craving for vengeance satisfied, and love
and sorrow triumphant—commits suicide, are set forth
in a manner equally touching and natural, and not, as
in the drama, sketched with a kind of panoramic roughness as part of a series of events chiefly affecting gods,
dwarfs, and giants. It may be asked why Wagner was not

satisfied with the human interest of these pathetic old chronicles? why he imposed upon them such a complicated supernatural apparatus, and made their characters and incidents help to grind out results with which, as a matter of necessity, they had nothing whatever to do? The true answer probably is that he sought to use the gods of Walhalla as the Greek dramatists employed the deities of Olympus, and thus to secure, if haply he might, the dignity, impressiveness, and "removedness" which distinguish the tragedies of antiquity. A test of his success may be applied in the form of two questions: first, have the incidents in *Der Ring des Nibelungen* the necessary breadth and importance? Secondly, has the drama a sufficiently high and obvious moral purport? The answers to these queries will decide whether Wagner's play is a childish fable or, in the highest sense, a work of art.

As regards the first point some standard of comparison is necessary, and I will take as such that other trilogy which 2,400 years ago was the talk of the civilised world, which also shows the supernatural arrayed against the supernatural, working through man as its agent, and which Wagner unquestionably had in mind when shaping his ponderous drama. Here we have in every scene the height of impressiveness, secured by events of commanding import set forth with perfect simplicity. In the *Agamemnon*, the return of the conqueror of Troy, his reception by

Clytemnestra, and presentation to her of Cassandra; the picture of the inspired prophetess as she sits alone in her chariot proclaiming the terrible deeds at hand, or calmly enters the palace to her death; the horror-inspiring cry of the murdered King, and the spectacle presented as the scene opens, revealing Clytemnestra, axe in hand, standing by her husband's corpse ready to justify the deed—all these things belong to the highest order of tragedy. Every action is weighty, every word to the purpose, every motive sufficient. Passing on to the *Cœphori*, we have the solemn meeting of Orestes and Electra at their father's tomb; the resolution to carry out Apollo's mandate of vengeance; the appearance of the disguised Orestes in the palace; the slaying of Clytemnestra and her paramour; the tableau of retribution when, as before, the scene opens showing the avenger standing, sword in hand, over his mother's body; and the beginning of his punishment as, pursued by the Furies, he rushes out, heedless whither. Following the stately march of the drama to its closing section, the *Eumenides*, we come upon the wonderful scene at the Delphian temple, the arousing of the sleeping Furies by the ghost of Clytemnestra, the trial and acquittal of Orestes by the Areopagus, and, lastly, the installation of the Furies, now become "kind ones," as protectors of Athens. All through this magnificent production of Greek art we are struck not by the beauty of its ideas and language alone, but also by its simple, massive, and imposing structure. Both the characters and scenes are few, but nothing is trivial, nor is there anywhere a descent from the loftiest height of grandeur, or the smallest abatement of overwhelming interest. Turning to *Der Ring des Nibelungen*, what a contrast is afforded! It is the vulgar bustle and glare of a pantomime "opening" compared with the classic beauty of the fairy scenes in *A Midsummer Night's Dream*. The stage swarms with gods, monsters, and human beings all playing at more or less undignified cross-purposes. Wotan, the god of gods, makes a bargain with giants, and trusts to the wiles of Loge for relief from its conditions. He plunders Alberich of the treasure, pays a debt with what is not his own, and, wanting to recover part of it, compromises with his conscience by raising up a hero who will do the deed for him. "Like master, like man," and I need not stop to point out how many of the scenes in which lesser personages figure are marked either by triviality or worse. That there are incidents and situations of poetic beauty, and even of grandeur, in the play cannot be denied, but they are few and far between as compared with those which excite ridicule or contempt. Some may urge that the drama faithfully reflects the mingled childishness and terrible beauty of Northern mythology; but I fail to discover any justification in the fact, especially as all of human interest and poetic attraction found in *Der Ring*

H

des Nibelungen exists in the primitive legends well-nigh
separate from Wagner's army of prosy gods and chattering
imps. Brought to the first test, therefore, the drama
fails. Let me now proceed to the second.

If Wagner aims to provide his countrymen with a
national form of art, he cannot complain when his
achievements are measured by the highest standard—when,
for example, we demand of him the obvious and lofty
moral significance apart from which a national drama,
considered as something beyond mere amusement, is like
salt that has lost its savour. The theatres of the Greeks
were temples of religion, their performances acts of the
utmost solemnity, their dramas lessons in the philosophy
of life or practical exemplifications of the ways of the gods
to man. Their poets spake in strophe and antistrophe as
men who discoursed of great and serious things, and no
Greek playgoer came from under the spell of Sophocles or
Euripides or Æschylus without matter for grave consideration. Thus must it be ever with a truly national drama
which exists for higher purposes than those served by a
pantomime or an *opéra-bouffe*. But what is the lofty
moral purport of *Der Ring des Nibelungen* to us who live in
the nineteenth century? What does it teach us? What
matter does it give us for profitable thought? Scenes of
murder, incest, theft, deceit, and vulgar trickery abound
in it. Why? The presentation of crime on the stage is

only justified by strong reasons; what are the reasons in Wagner's case? Are they summed up in a desire to show that the rule of love is stronger than that of force, or that the pursuit of power leads through devious and dirty ways? If so the lesson is almost lost in the complexity of the fable. Surely it was not needful to take up four evenings, and parade thirty-four gods, giants, imps, and mortals, for such an elementary purpose. We lose the moral in the machinery which works it out, and when it is considered that almost the entire *dramatis personæ* are to us abstractions, while the conditions under which they exist are beyond our realisation, the fact may even be that we remain insensible to the presence of any moral at all. The conclusion is unavoidable that Wagner's drama lacks the most essential qualities of its order. It neither impresses us by the breadth and grandeur of its scenes, nor conveys eternal truths to our minds with the directness and simplicity of which the stage is capable in a degree unknown elsewhere.

Oct. 7.

Having discussed the poem of *Der Ring des Nibelungen* as regards the character of its subject, I have now to look at it as a drama intended for association with music. In doing this it is no part of my purpose to follow Wagner through his elaborate and involved dissertations upon the relative position and privileges of allied poetry and music. Amateurs who take any sort of interest in the question are more or less familiar with his line of argument; while those who know nothing about it may have reason to believe, before I conclude, that from a practical point of view their ignorance is no serious matter. It will suffice for the purpose of this criticism if I examine Wagner's drama to see how it carries out his cardinal doctrine that poetry must yield nothing to music, and, apart from a necessary "yearning" for musical expression, is independent of it. A glance at *Der Ring des Nibelungen* shows that the master has not shrunk from giving a practical illustration of this theory in its fullest and most rigid sense. Nobody expected that he would. Wagner ever has the courage of his opinions, and, what is more, is always ready not only to avow but to act up to them. Here, nevertheless, it is easy to imagine that Wagner the poet must have been strongly opposed by Wagner the musician, since the first so disregarded the second as to lay upon him a task obviously more than even his gigantic strength and indomitable resolution could achieve. Under ordinary circumstances the poet arranges his drama with at least provision for the orderly and effective sequence of recitative, solo, concerted piece, and orchestral interlude. Till Wagner proclaimed his latest theories this concession from the one art to the other was looked upon as a matter of course, involving no loss of dignity to the conceder, who simply met one of the requirements of an honourable alliance. Doubtless in many cases the poet has yielded to the musician far more than he ought; but the fact remains that the most illustrious examples of musico-dramatic art are formed upon the principle, unquestioned by their authors, that he must grant at least as much as I have stated. Leaving out of present consideration the yearning after musical expression which he admits that "lines for music" should have, it may be said that Wagner grants nothing. The poet of music-drama is, with him, absolutely a free and independent worker, responsible only to the rules of his own art, and even as regards them, if we may judge by *Der Ring des Nibelungen*, revelling in the full liberty of the epic, rather than restrained by dramatic exigencies. Here the question arises, Is the poet's absolute disregard of the musician an essential demand of perfected music-drama? If so there is no more to be said, because the most rabid opponent of Wagner must acknowledge that the thing illustrated is superior to its illustration, just as a thing shadowed is superior to its shadow. It follows that a music-drama cannot forego any dramatic essential for music's sake without becoming, like so many operatic libretti, an object of just ridicule. But, while frankly admitting this, it may be contended that there is a middle course between such an offence against obvious law and

the extreme path chosen by Wagner when, as a poet, he
resolved upon yielding nothing to the claims of the sister
art. That middle course, it appears to me, Wagner himself has marked out in *Der Fliegende Holländer*, which I
cite by preference because so many English amateurs
have lately enjoyed an opportunity of making its acquaintance. The poem of *Der Fliegende Holländer* is as full and
perfect a drama as need be wished. Its story is simple
and readily comprehended, its scenes are each animated
by a well-marked purpose, and its dialogue has all necessary completeness. In point of fact Wagner's taste and
skill as a dramatic author shine nowhere with a steadier
light than in his treatment of the grim sea-legend. Yet
the excellence of *Der Fliegende Holländer* as a play appears
in conjunction with due provision for the essential requirements of music. It allows of song, duet, trio, and chorus
almost as readily as the absurd concoctions of men who
have written with an eye to music alone ; and thus, while
the mind is gratified by the presentation of a complete
drama on the one hand, on the other it derives pleasure
from music based upon true and acknowledged artistic
principles. These are facts not to be disputed as such,
and not to be obscured by the most intricate network of
Wagnerian phrases. It follows that a drama for music
constructed on a radically different basis should offer well-
marked and important advantages before meeting with

acceptance. Do we find such advantages in *Der Ring des Nibelungen*? That is the crucial question to which an answer must be supplied.

What then are the chief constructive features of *Der Ring des Nibelungen*? First of all, an elaboration of dialogue and scene which makes the application of music in its acknowledged forms a sheer impossibility. Not only so, but the application of music in any form would *primâ facie* strike the mind as opposed to the author's design. "This is a drama to be read," so would the conclusion run, "or mayhap played, where the difficulties of its *mise-en-scène* can be got over." Let me prove the natural- ness of the judgment by help of some details taken almost at random from various portions of the work. The first scene in *Die Walküre* shows the meeting of Siegmund and Sieglinde, and sets forth the poetical incidents leading up to an example of "purely human" action in the form of incest. Here, amid much that is beautifully treated, the necessities of Wagner's system compel a fulness of verbal utterance which sets the musician at defiance.

"Make me glad of my guest,"

says Hunding, the husband of Sieglinde;

"Give me notice now of his name."

In reply, Siegmund takes up no fewer than 108 lines with an autobiographical sketch. The same hero, when left alone by his sister and the man whom she intends to drug in order to "carry on" with the stranger guest, muses in fifty-eight lines, and Sieglinde's first speech to him after her return occupies sixty-eight. The second act of the same section of the drama is wholly devoted to dialogue, first between Wotan and his wife Fricka, next between the same garrulous god and his daughter Brünnhilde. Dialogue No. 1 contains 229 lines, the larger share of which, by right of her sex, belongs to Fricka, whose chief speech takes up fifty-two lines. One might imagine that after this Wagner provides some relief, but the stern dramatist goes calmly on to the 326 lines of dialogue No. 2. Here Wotan, comparatively reticent in presence of his wife, indulges to the full a love for long stories, which, although they convey information to Brünnhilde, tell us nothing we do not already know. Two of these utterances are respectively seventy-eight lines long, and a third extends to forty-five. Similar examples might be adduced till they become as wearisome as Wotan himself—and that is saying much; but enough if I have given an idea of the form in which Wagner works as a dramatic poet. That form is obviously not compatible with orthodox music, but the point need not be insisted upon, since Wagner never so intended. The question is whether any musician could possibly illustrate in any way such a text with a satisfactory artistic result. To answer this the character as well as the form of the poetry must be taken into account.

I have already remarked that Wagner attaches one condition to words for music—they must yearn after musical expression. This, of course, is no new discovery, and, indeed, orthodox composers of dramatic music have recognised and acted upon the fact with more completeness than Wagner himself. The lyrical element in libretti is a distinct homage to the requirements which Wagner formulates; as is, no less, the practice of setting ordinary dialogue to recitative. More, the desire for such "yearning" words often prompts libretti-makers to go absurdly out of the direct path of the drama in order to find them. But, inasmuch as Wagner subjects the entire drama to the same form of musical expression, it follows that every part of it must stand in need of that which such musical expression supplies. Does *Der Ring des Nibelungen* meet this condition? Let us ascertain by dipping here and there into the body of the work for a sample.

When in *Das Rheingold* Alberich pursues the Rhine Daughters, he exclaims,—

> " Sleek as slime
> the slope of the slate is !
> I slant and slide ;
> With foot and with fist
> I can fix myself not
> on the slippery surface.   [*He sneezes.*
> Floods of wet
> flow in my nostrils ;
> the cursèd coughing !

Does the dialogue, of which this is a fair specimen, yearn for

musical expression?   Again, when Freia is taken away by
the giants, and the gods begin to look old, Loge speaks :—

> " How poor and pale
> you suddenly seem !
> All your cheeks have lost their light;
> the look of your eyes is allayed !
> Up, my Froh,
> it's early yet !
> In thy hand, Donner,
> how fares with thy hammer?
> What frightens Fricka ?
> Greets she not gladly
> the greyness Wotan has got
> that makes him quite an old man ? "

Would anybody ever feel a prompting to sing these lines ?
Once more Alberich, in altercation with his brother Mime,
snarls,—

> " For his kindly care
> will the niggardly
> nasty old knave—
> bold and base—
> now be nothing but King ?
> The mangiest dog
> might for the hoop
> be meeter than he ;
> hope not to have
> thy hand on its mastering gold !"

It is useless to multiply such instances, for these are
fair selections from a crowd of passages which, however
excellent as belonging to the drama—that point is not in
question—have scarcely more essential connection with
music than a table of logarithms.   The objection, be it
noted, is not that Wagner introduces such lines into his

play, seeing that these, or others analogous to them, could not well be kept out. It is rather that Wagner insists on their being regarded as suggestive of music, and so endeavours to establish a principle which would place the dramatic composer under burdens too grievous to be borne. Seeing then that both the form, and in many cases the character, of Wagner's poem are at variance with the universally accepted necessities of artistic music—seeing also that this is not a result of dramatic exigencies, but of a strained theory—the rejection of *Der Ring des Nibelungen* as a model music-drama becomes inevitable. But it would be unfair not to acknowledge the many passages in all sections of the work from which, so to speak, music naturally springs. Page after page might be quoted wherein true poetic feeling abounds, and it is precisely in these instances that Wagner, overcoming the obstacles presented by his own musical system, is musically successful. Otherwise, not even his genius and will have been able to avoid failure.

Among the master's dramatic theories is one to the effect that nothing in a stage-play should be left to intellectual perception, the appeal being only to emotions, acting without disturbance from mental exercise. I do not mean to discuss this principle, but merely to point out the result of its operation in music-drama, that result being, as I think, extremely disastrous. In proportion to

the elaborate character of a given story are its demands
upon perceptiveness; and where perceptiveness is fore-
stalled, in proportion also must be the fulness of its
exhibition to the senses. Wagner carries this out with
unmerciful scrupulousness in every part of *Der Ring des
Nibelungen*. Each section is within its limits a complete
thing, and the relation of incidents already known
necessarily therefore takes up a great part of all except
the first. Character after character comes on with a long
story of past, and to those whose vision extends over the
whole drama familiar, events. Thus, in *Die Walküre*,
Wotan sketches to Brünnhilde the entire plot up to the
point at which he speaks. In *Siegfried* Mime reveals to
the hero secrets which are no secrets to us; Wotan and
Mime speak together at inordinate length of events fresh
in our recollection; and in his interview with Erda
Wotan repeats the story of Brünnhilde's disobedience and
punishment which we saw enacted in *Die Walküre*. In
Götterdämmerung the Norns begin with a kind of general
survey of the whole position; Hagen tells of Siegfried's
birth and achievements, as set forth in the previous
sections; Alberich rehearses to Hagen more of the hero's
well-known deeds, and Siegfried himself repeats the story
in full just previous to his death. There is no getting
away from this biographical fever, and at every fresh
entrance of a leading character we wait in dread for a

sensation kindred to that which pervades a theatre when chairs are brought down to the lamps and a voice begins, "It is now some thirty years ago," &c. From a dramatic point of view this repetition of long stories is terribly wearisome, but upon the musician it presses hardly indeed, burdening him with a lot of stale matter that necessarily involves a tremendous strain upon his imagination, or, as in Wagner's case, taxes his ingenuity for the means of presenting old themes in varied forms, while leaving him hopeless of recommending by his art that with which his art has been in most cases unnecessarily connected.

Even the foregoing cursory examination of Wagner's drama as a poem for music gives a sufficiently vivid idea of the manner in which the claims of music are ignored, and it is unnecessary to dwell upon such points as its uniformity of rhythm and the frequent harshness of its alliterative lines. But, wholly setting aside matters of theory, the question should be asked whether Wagner's severe regard for that which he looks upon as dramatic truth does not ignore a grand fact impossible to be reasoned away by any number of pamphlets. Marvellous and beautiful systems have been thought out by workers in all branches of intellectual labour; but a moment's contact with the everyday world has toppled many of them over, as the disinterred body of a long-dead man crumbles into dust at the touch of light and air. So may it be with Wagner's theory of the absolute subjection of music to poetry. Admitting that, as a theory, no flaw exists in it, the all-important question is, " Will it work ? " I answer, " Yes, when the positions instinctively assigned to the allied arts are reversed; when the language of poetry exerts greater and readier power than that of music ; when the poet can stir the emotions and kindle the imagination more easily than the musician; when Orpheus soothes ' the inexorable powers of hell ' with declamation instead of song, and David, leaving his harp at the palace-gate, appeases the fiend of melancholy Saul with a volume of ' Elegant Extracts.' " But the time for this change is not yet. Was the gathering at Bayreuth a gathering of dramatists or musicians ? For what, before all other, had the crowded theatre ears ? Of what was the chief discourse ? The only possible reply expresses a truth firm-based in the very nature of things. You cannot change that truth by theorising; and wherever music and poetry are associated, there will the more universal and mightier art prevail. He who ignores this fact, to the degradation of music, does so at his peril. He may build a towering fabric for the great of the earth to gather round with admiring eyes, but he builds on sand. Sooner or later comes a crash; men clear away a heap of rubbish, and the world goes calmly on to higher things.

Appendix.

THE TOWN OF HANS SACHS.

A JOURNEY, the object of which is Bayreuth, what time Wagner exhibits the "Art-Work of the Future" in his Nibelungen trilogy, cannot do better than have Nuremberg for its first stage. We are told that the Festival Play in the little town over yonder is to be not only the apotheosis of an essentially German musician and poet, but the inauguration of a new art-era for the Fatherland; Germany, through it, becoming the happy possessor of a music-drama the ownership of which none could dispute, if any were inclined to try. As a preparation for this event a foreigner should Teutonize himself somewhat. He cannot be expected, unless he do so, to get into sympathy with the occasion. What, to such an unprepared one, is the Nibelungen legend but a grotesque old story, on a par with the veracious chronicles of the Seven Champions of Christendom? In his case, small indeed is the power of recognizing that at least one form of national art should rest upon myths and fables, however childish or absurd, or of discerning that, if you only look at these things through

I

proper spectacles, they are seen to have a wonderful and subtle faculty of regenerating the human mind. To appreciate what is coming at Bayreuth, therefore, one must breathe the atmosphere of German art, but not, be it well understood, the art of modern Germany. Though Wagner may succeed in laying a foundation for the future, he himself, and his method of working, belong to the far past. In some respects he brings to mind the stout old heroes among whom the city in which I write numbers so many sons. True, *they* were content to labour silently for the love of what they did, and for the glory of Him who is the Giver of all good gifts; whereas Wagner resembles the familiar bird which cannot lay an egg without making a " communication to its friends " and the world in general about the fact. But, noisy self-assertion apart, the author of the *Nibelungen* has a good deal of the antique German spirit in him. That he lives and moves among German traditions everybody knows, while, with regard to his latest music, one may look upon it as analogous to the creations, half-grotesque, half-heroic, of Gothic fancy. With all this in mind, I cannot help thinking that Wagner should have chosen Nuremberg for his festival. It may be objected that the old town is now chiefly associated with so-called Dutch toys and bad blacklead pencils; but the Nuremberg of the present matters not. Enough that here we have the birthplace and nursery of much that is best in German art;

and that the history of this whilom Free City is a record
to be looked upon by every Teuton with pride—not to
mention the fact that Wagner himself has made Nuremberg
the scene of the only opera in which he illustrates the
peculiarly cumbrous mental exercise resulting in German
humour.

There is a fine flavour of the Middle Ages about Nuremberg. The nineteenth century beleaguers the city, it is
true, screaming at it with railway whistles from outside
the ditch, and mocking its antique grandeur with very
modern suburbs. But the old place, serene within
encircling walls and embattled towers, looks calmly on.
The nineteenth century has small chance inside. You
leave it at the gateway as a Mohammedan worshipper puts
off his slippers in the porch, nor does it much signify that
the people about the streets wear a garb belonging to the
present day. The "local colour" is too strong for any such
evidence that we are not exactly in the fifteenth century;
chimney-pot hats are overshadowed by the gables upon
which the eyes of Albert Dürer lovingly rested, and quaint
old Gothic saints and devils extinguish the cut-away coat.
What is equally to the purpose, Nuremberg preserves its
antique air of repose. The hurry and bustle of a modern
city would not do for it at all—cannot live here, in point
of fact—so along the streets such carriages as the needs of
the place require serenely move, varied now and then by a

cart which a couple of bullocks have placidly agreed to draw on condition of choosing their own pace. But this, and much more like it, is a matter of course. Every scene has its peculiar influence, and Nuremberg, with magic power, puts the timepiece of the Ages back a few hundred years in the feeling of, at all events, the stranger within its gates. The stout old burghers, whose enterprise made "Nuremberg's hand go through every land," still walk the streets, visible to the eye of the dullest fancy. Albert Dürer is yet busy at his easel in the house near the Thiergarten Thor up yonder; Adam Krafft is labouring at his reliefs for the Stations of the Cross, ordered by pious Martin Ketzel, who has journeyed to the Holy Land and brought back the exact distances; while Peter Vischer, with his five sons, working, as he himself said, "for the praise of God Almighty alone and the honour of St. Sebaldus, Prince of Heaven," have just completed the wondrous shrine before which every pilgrim bows, in reverent admiration of patient toil and masterful art. These men, and such as they—Veit Stoss, Wohlgemuth, Hirschvogel—are the actual citizens of Nuremberg. You cannot get away from them. On Dürer's tomb in St. John's churchyard some one wrote "Emigravit," and Longfellow has said :—

"Emigravit" is the inscription on the tombstone where he lies;
Dead he is not, but departed—for the artist never dies.

Both the inscription and the poet are wrong. The old Nuremberg masters are as really present here as ever they were, so true is it that an artist's work is the best and most essential part of him. What grand old fellows they are! How earnest and thorough! How childlike, yet how heroic! In fancy, what a mixture of the grotesque and the noble, and in all things how real, never averse from calling a spade a spade! There is a picture in St. Siebald's Church, by some unknown hand of, it is said, the twelfth century, which, perhaps, best illustrates this strange commingling. It is a Crucifixion, and the noble, patient, suffering face of the victim brings tears to the eyes, at the same time that the horrible truth of the whole inclines one to turn away in disgust and pain. Although the painter could give us that face, he knew nothing of idealizing his subject, and as a natural result we have the blood-stained body, anguish-torn, the muscles of the poor arms standing out like cords, while along the hollows thus made a red stream flows from the pierced hands. A few yards away stands the Vischer shrine to illustrate the fancy which these strong workers cultivated along with their realism. That the whole masterpiece of metal-work rests upon snails, above which are dolphins, above which are the Twelve Apostles, with an infant Christ on the top of all, excites no surprise; but the artist has thrown in a multitude of little winged boys, cherubs or cupids, engaged in various ways, more or less inappropriate. One has injured his toe, and contemplates it ruefully; another weeps for an apple which a third has snatched; and everywhere the little fellows exhibit a want of reverence for the saintly relics behind them such as moves the gravest to laughter. But Nuremberg artists could be grimly as well as sportively humorous. Over a church porch here there is a representation of the Last Judgment, showing a procession of ecclesiastics moving complacently towards heaven, while certain Jews, Turks, and infidels are being dragged the other way by a powerful and highly elate demon, who has wound a chain round the whole of them. Such things are common, but not so the touch—of satire is it?—shown where the last of the saved answers the appeal of the rearmost lost one with a vigorous push in the direction of the "pit." So through the whole range of Nuremberg art are discernible the odd quips and cranks of Gothic fancy, in union with Gothic strength and grandeur. Was I not right, therefore, in saying that this wonderful old city is a good preparative for the cognate phenomena promised us at Bayreuth?

But, amid a crowd of claims upon his attention, the musical visitor is not likely to forget that Nuremberg is the city of Hans Sachs—the home, if not the birthplace, of the Master-singers. How that remarkable guild arose from the ruins of the Minnegesang practised by the noble and courtly poets of an earlier time no man knows. But all traditions ascribe its origin, in great measure, to popular as distinct from patrician genius—of the twelve Master-singers said to have arisen in the thirteenth century, one being a glass-blower, another a smith, another a fisherman, and another a rope-maker. Whatever the facts of earlier times, it is certain that the guild was incorporated by the Emperor Charles IV. in 1387, and that from the parent school at Mayence branches spread all over Germany. Of these the last to perish had its seat in Nuremberg, where the influence of Sachs's fame and works made a good fight against time and change. Nuremberg is thus, in more than one respect, closely associated with the Master-singers, and the church in which they met as late as the year 1770 may claim to have been their special temple. As regards their influence upon German art, much cannot be said. Like most guilds of the kind, they elevated the form above the spirit, loaded the practice of their craft with cumbersome and senseless rules, and so degraded it that a mere capacity of imitation sufficed to meet the requirements of membership. One cannot resist a smile at the spectacle presented by the Nuremberg church with the Master-singers in council. A low platform enclosed by curtains served for the functionary who marked the faults of the candidates ; on the benches surrounding it sat the masters, solemnly critical; and in a place apart stood the aspirant whose observance of rhyme and rattle, rather than whose poetic spirit, gave occasion for judgment. Generally, indeed, the measure and melody had to be approved before the "poet" was allowed to write a line, so complete was the bondage imposed by the guild-rules. Thirty-three faults were allowed at Nuremberg; whoever exceeded that number failing to pass the ordeal, all others winning a Master's seat. In the "Freisingen," which must have been by far the more interesting exercise, all were allowed to join, provided the themes were based upon Holy Writ or "true and honourable profane mundane events together with good moral maxims." That the institution kept alive a certain spirit of culture by such practices may be a fact; but its influence over the masses—who had their own song, from which German poetry, as we know it, arose—could never have been great. Hans Sachs, it is true, was a power; not, however, because he held high rank among the Master-singers. The racy, homely utterances of the cobbler poet reached the hearts of the people by the shortest route, and would have done so in any case, for he was an artist sent on a mission which he discharged with the instinct of genius first, and only in the second place with reference to rule and order. Thanks to this, Hans Sachs makes the most considerable figure among the Master-singers, shedding upon his guild a glory of which it has none too much. In return, Nuremberg is proud of Hans Sachs—not, however, to the extent of purchasing his house and consecrating it to his memory. A wine merchant lives on the spot where the poet hammered his leather and composed his songs; but the street is named after him, which is something, and the house-front bears aloft a portrait of the staunch old hero. Thither go visitors from every land, some mayhap, as myself, afterwards following the route by which they bore his body along the Via Dolorosa of Adam Krafft, past the Calvary, and so to the Golgotha where it now rests. Sachs lies among a crowd of the old patrician burghers, whose massive monuments are covered with heraldic insignia and pompous epitaphs, executed in ironwork such as might have come from the foundry of Vischer. But the poet's grave is not thus marked. He had no coat of arms, and was entitled to quarter nothing that a herald's college would recognize. The visitor, nevertheless, turns his back upon the Nuremberg nobility with all their *post-mortem* grandeur, and has eyes only for the grave of the poor cobbler. So in the long run is Wisdom justified of her children.

Upon the whole town rests the glamour of that which we fondly regard as an heroic age; but should there be in this any sort of danger to the enthusiastic visitor, let him go to a certain tower on the wall and contemplate the choice assortment of articles thought necessary to mediæval government. The Iron Virgin will be enough to set matters right. Nuremberg, true to its traditions, had a grimly humorous way of adjusting its disputes with troublesome people. The Virgin took them to her embrace, and a few minutes later dropped them into oblivion through a convenient trap-door. Nuremberg preserves the Virgin (not for use), and also certain full-flavoured smells, the tendency of which is to reconcile the most enthusiastic *laudator temporis acti* to the prosaic character of modern civilization.

THE BIRTHPLACE OF MOZART.

SALZBURG, AUGUST 1.

THE Prince-Archbishop of Salzburg was a potential individual in the olden time. He held his head high among the
grandees of the Empire. Two hundred thousand souls owned
him for their temporal as well as spiritual chief, and he could
at a pinch—having exchanged the mitre for the helmet—
lead 6,000 men into the field. Everywhere in his own
dominions he was a very great man indeed, and did mighty
things. He built churches enough to make every in-
habitant a saint; erected splendid fountains; bored
tunnels through rocks, and carved his name at each
entrance; looked after the welfare of his people with the
birch-rod of paternal discipline in his hand, and permitted
nobody to do or say anything opposed to his reverend and
orthodox judgment. There were times, it is true, when
this embodiment of a united Church and State was not
happy. Perverse generations arose with the audacity
to think that the Prince-Archbishop was an abatable
nuisance, under which impression they did their utmost

to get rid of him. But his sacerdotal Highness enjoyed
the luck of a personage who could not possibly have been
his master, and by some means or other—occasionally by
battering the town with cannon—held on to dignity and
power, spending, on the whole, a good time in the castle
with which, to be as near heaven as possible without
quitting earth, he had crowned the highest adjacent hill.
From his proud place of Hohensalzburg, the Prince-
Archbishop looked down upon the town in a double sense,
and might have been forgiven the thought that, under no
conceivable circumstances, could a greater man than himself arise within its limits. Imagine the feelings of the
reverend and puissant gentleman had some far-seer—say
Theophrastus Paracelsus, who died in a house just across
the river—found audience for words like these: "May it
please your Highness's Grace, the time is approaching when
Salzburg will have but a shadowy Prince-Archbishop, when
this your castle will be a barrack, and when from all parts
of the world pilgrims will flock to see here the birthplace
of the son of a poor musician." The result of such a fore-
cast would, probably, have been the prophet's acquaintance
with some of the ingenious mechanical appliances used in
Salzburg to supplement the anathemas of the Church. But
the gift of second sight may have belonged also to the great
man, in which case he would have replied : " Your hero of
the future will live in poverty, die young, and be buried in

a nameless grave. What has the Prince-Archbishop of Salzburg to fear from his rivalry?" Nevertheless, at this day Salzburg belongs to the son of the poor musician. Mozart is the true Prince of the beautiful little city, and, by comparison, the dignitaries who lived in the castle above are a mere sequence of sounding but empty names. You cannot walk about the streets without constantly recognizing the supremacy of the divine master. The people talk of Mozart as though conscious that the thought of him is uppermost in your mind; his *spirituel* face meets the eye in countless windows; tradesmen carry on their business under the shadow of his name; his melodies ring out from the campaniles of the churches; after him public places are called; and in the very centre of the town his statue stands like that of a king—the effigy of one whom, indeed, kings have, on that same spot, delighted to honour. The Prince-Archbishop is nowhere by comparison. In front of the cathedral one sees a stone figure, robed and mitred, dirty, time-worn, and with no face to speak of. That represents the present state of the whole line of clerico-secular dignities. The passing years have battered their memorials, and nobody cares a jot about them.

"Mozart's Geburtshaus"—the inscription stares you in the face as you pass through the old archway near the bridge and advance towards a line of five-storied dwellings forming one side of a narrow street, known as Getreide

Gasse. In 1756 the Mozarts—Mozart *père* being, as everybody knows, Kapellmeister to the Prince-Archbishop—
tenanted the third floor of this residence. It is a large
house, and at present contains more than one family,
unless, indeed, the grocer, to whose trade the ground floor
is devoted, makes abundant profit, and has a big establishment. Whether the Kapellmeister rented any other part
than the story over the front windows of which a gilded
lyre now shines may be doubted. His family was small,
his salary not great, and his disposition inclined rather
to the accumulation of money than to spending it for
any purpose that was not strictly essential. We may
assume, therefore, that the Mozarts lived exclusively on
the third floor, and that in one of the rooms facing the
street happened, 120 years ago, the event which gave to
the world of music its most perfect artist, and to the lovers
of beauty an unfailing source of pleasure. A lowly place
was that wherein the wonder-child first saw the light; but
there is a dignity about it now such as cannot be associated even with palaces—a dignity so easy of reflection
that some of it shines in the face of the grocer, and attracts
to him our regards. Surely all the musical inhabitants of
Salzburg buy their tea and coffee at "Mozart's Geburtshaus"! Property, we often hear, has its duties; but it
has also its rights, and one of them is the right of quiet
enjoyment. I have not, therefore, ventured to intrude

upon the inhabitants of the third floor. Wishing them joy
of so distinguished a residence, it would hardly be consistent to help in worrying them out of it. For the same
reason do I respect the threshold of the one-story dwelling
in Hannibal Platz, on the front of which is writ large,
"Mozart's Wohnhaus." The elder Mozart must have
prospered at Salzburg before he could have ventured to
move from the Getreide Gasse to that which is, by comparison, a mansion. It appears that he tenanted no more
than a wing; but the building covers a great extent of
ground, there being on the upper floor no fewer than
eleven windows. Entrance is gained to the place through
an archway, and the entire edifice has an antique, sub-
stantial, and highly-respectable appearance. That it is
well cared for a glance suffices to show. Flowers bloom in
the windows, the house-front is bright and clean, and a
fine old-fashioned air of repose is given to it by the quaint
and quiet Platz in which it stands. Here, then, is the
home of the great composer—the spot to which, amid
many wanderings, his affectionate nature turned with constant delight. It was to this house that the letters came
which are now read by the world—letters full of dutiful
affection to an exacting father, charged with a million
kisses to the mother, or bright with sportive messages to
the sister. We can fancy with what joy those epistles
were received, for we know how carefully they were pre-

served, and one likes to imagine even the pedantic Kapellmeister, who meets the postman in going to mass, retracing
his steps, at the risk of being late for the "Kyrie," that he
might share Wolfgang's news with his family. Beyond
this *bourgeois* residence and the modest lodging in
Vienna, Mozart never rose, so that there is a mighty
step from his condition during life to that represented
here by the Platz named after him and the kingly statue
which lifts its proud head in the centre. The key to the
change is, of course, in everybody's hands, and was im-
pressively suggested to me last Sunday morning, when
passing the open doors of the ornate Italian church which
does duty as a cathedral. Sounds of solemn music floated
out into the open, and a little crowd of idlers, revelling in
the shade of the building, listened and looked as, at the far
end of the interior, clouds of incense obscured the lighted
altar and half hid the resplendent forms of the priests.
The spectacle is common enough to travellers in Catholic
lands, but here it had at least one feature of rare significance, for the beautiful music that filled the vast church
came from the genius of Mozart. Deeply as the congrega-
tion may have felt the influence of the moment, they could
hardly estimate the effect upon a stranger, who, familiar
with the Mass in B flat from childhood, listened to its
"Sanctus" in the building for which the master wrote,
and surrounded by memorials of his career. Under no

other circumstances could the music have had such power, or have been more fully able to account for the transition from poverty and neglect to the homage of a world.

What so natural as that Salzburg should possess many and priceless relics of its illustrious son? These, as most people in England know—thanks to the performance given by Madame Adelina Patti at the Royal Italian Opera a few years ago, in aid of the Mozarteum here—are the property of an institution which seeks to honour the great composer chiefly by training others to follow the art he adorned. There is reason to believe that the laudable enterprise is not supported to the full extent of its merits, but it has, at least, succeeded in filling one small room with greater interest than belongs to all the neighbouring palaces put together. The Mozarteum cannot yet boast a local habitation of its own, and its relics are to be found in an antique mansion forming part of an obscure bye-street. Passing under an archway, the visitor ascends to the first floor, where, if he be keen-sighted enough to observe certain faint directions, he may at length find himself in an apartment strongly suggestive of a curiosity shop. On my entrance, the sole occupant was a little man, who sprang briskly up with a hurried salutation. rushed to a harpsichord, seated himself, and saying, "This is Mozart's concert instrument," began to play "La ci darem." I don't know whether the little man desired to

K

impress me by a sort of *tour de force*, but it soon appeared
that he gave everybody an exactly similar reception. On
each visitor's arrival he would dart to the harpsichord and
plunge into the familiar duet, afterwards going through
his round of description with unabated enthusiasm for
the subject, laughing as heartily at things and events as
though they were to him perfectly fresh and new. He had
much to show besides the quaint harpsichord with its feeble
tinkle. Mozart's spinet stands close at hand—a feebler
machine still, and one adapted to please Othello, as making
"music which may not be heard." Hanging on the walls
are original portraits of the Mozart family, from the composer's grandmother down to his sons, including Constance
Weber and her second husband, Von Nissen. Beneath
one small likeness of the great man himself is placed a
lock of his hair—very dark brown—and near it is a drawing
of his ear, showing an abnormally large "bell," as though
nature intended him to be a gifted listener. An *affiche*
of the first performance of *Die Zauberflöte* is also exhibited, together with a little song (MS.), the words as
well as the music of which were written by Mozart—
his only appearance in a double capacity. Among other
treasures are piles of original letters, numerous MS.
compositions, Mozart's album, his ring, watch appendages,
snuff-box, and pocket-book—a somewhat dandy article,
containing, one is surprised to find, a label marked

"Genuine Court Plaster, London." Was, then, Court plaster among the exports of the British metropolis, or did Mozart purchase the article during his visit to England? Furthermore, what did he do with it? Could he not handle his razor deftly? or had he a taste for "beauty spots?" Anyhow there are the dandy pocket-book, the London court plaster, the ring, the watch ornament—a ponderous affair—and the really handsome snuff-box, equipped with which, and perhaps a "clouded cane," our Mozart must have made a respectable figure, even outside the realms of genius. On the whole, and considering the difficulty of obtaining such relics, the Mozarteum has done well. As years jog on, it may do better, and accumulate under one roof every important thing deriving its interest from personal association with the illustrious composer.

I did not intend making any reference in this letter to the aspect of the town and neighbourhood, but it deserves to be pointed out how the scenes amid which Mozart spent his youthful years must have had no small influence in stimulating that sense of the beautiful which his works so perfectly display. Here he saw beauty all around—a wonderful combination of mountain and valley, hill and plain, rushing river and quiet lake, hoary castle and solemn church, quaint streets and blooming gardens, waving woods and smiling meadows. Nothing was wanting to the splendour and loveliness of the pictures upon which his young eyes rested, we would fain believe, with constant pleasure. Mozart is gone—if, indeed, that may be said of him—but the pictures remain; and it is right that scenes so exquisite should be for ever associated with the memory of one who was a master of beauty.

THREE FAMOUS GRAVES.

To the musical visitor, Vienna, with all its magnificence, is a place of graves. Notable things are done there now in opera-house and concert-room; composers may still be found there of whom the great world outside has heard; but the artistic glory of the capital chiefly illumines the cemeteries outside its walls. Gluck, Haydn, Mozart, Beethoven, Schubert lie in death around the city on which they helped to confer an immortality more precious than any arising from deeds of arms, from European congresses or imperial splendours; and no one with musical sympathies can rest in Vienna long before making a pilgrimage to the shrines, for ever sacred, where reposes "all of *genius* that could die."

It was a scorching August day when I came out from under the protecting shadow of St. Stephen's to search for the grave of Mozart. I had lingered long in the coolness and solitude of the Chapel of the Cross, where the final benediction was pronounced over the composer's body; and my route was that taken by the poor, scanty, and straggling procession to the burial-ground of St. Marx, far away outside the Maria Hilf lines. Funeral trains were still passing, perhaps to the same destination, but under how different circumstances! As I walked in the sunlight amid the bustle and animation of a great city, which, not less than Paris, seems in such glorious weather to breathe the very atmosphere of gaiety, it was impossible not to contrast the scene with that presented on the stormy December day when Mozart took his last sad journey. I could picture the sorry sight—one that must sting the conscience of humanity as long as any sense of feeling remains. As the coffin is borne out of the cathedral in the pouring rain numbers who have attended the service disappear round the angles of the building and are seen no more. Others, faithful for the nonce, shelter themselves beneath umbrellas and accompany the remains along the muddy streets, but even these cannot hold out to the end. "They all forsook him and fled." There was not even "that other disciple" to "follow him afar off." So, unattended, save by hirelings, the body was carried forth into the dismal country and laid in the common grave.

Passing the "lines" in the direction of the cemetery, it appeared as though a malicious fate persecuted the composer even after burial. What may have been the immediate surroundings of St. Marx ninety years ago can now only be guessed. Let us hope that there were meadows, and trees, and singing birds; that flowers bloomed in rich profusion, and that over all reigned the peace of nature. But, if so, nothing of it remains. Vienna has grown, till now the burial-ground is an oasis in the desert which a great city makes of the quarters it ultimately means to cover with houses or devote to its many needs. To the left is a huge cattle-market, where Hungarian graziers drive hard bargains with Vienna butchers, who doubtless take revenge on their own customers. Away to the right is a big barrack, noisy with words of command and rifle-practice. Parallel with the road runs a dirty canal bordered by straggling houses; while even up to the cemetery walls extends a waste, amid which excavators and lime-burners ply their trade. Those who remember the neighbourhood of Copenhagen Fields when first given up to the men "whose talk is about bullocks" may form some idea of the scenes amid which Mozart reposes. But once inside the hallowed inclosure all these things are forgotten. The entrance, situated in low ground by the canal-side, has a quaint homely aspect, with its unpretending gate and guardian's lodge, on each side of which a few humble vendors of flowers and *immortelles* expose their goods for sale.

St. Marx is clearly not a fashionable cemetery, for as I enter it, glad to find a place of rest and shelter from the heat, I seem to be alone with the dead. Actually, however, there is life about—the life that lives on death. In the distance I see a man tending a grave. He is a feeble old fellow, who stops now and then to straighten his back and wipe his perspiring face. As he does this on one occasion he observes my presence, and, with the unvarying courtesy of an Austrian, gives me "good day." I return the wish, and ask for information as to Mozart's grave. The old man leans upon a tomb and reflects as though he had heard the name of Mozart, but was uncertain in what connection. "Mozart! Mozart!" he mutters, and thinks desperately hard, but to no purpose. Then he shouts "Max," and a response comes out of the earth a few yards off. Max is digging, and I see his sunburnt face turned towards us from a fresh-raised mound. "Where is Mozart's grave?" queries the old man. By this time Max has put a bottle to his lips, which he removes only so long as is necessary to answer, "Tell the Herr to look among the little crosses." The old man bends painfully down to his task again, and I move up the gentle slope of the avenue in search of "little crosses." Still up and up among the tombs of the Viennese burghers; but the crosses are all big. At last, there are the small ones! acres of them rising above the rank grass as though the ground had brought them forth like weeds, and gay in many places with tawdry tributes of affection. Turning aside, I wander amongst them, reading on every hand "the short and simple annals of the poor," and am thus engaged when I come full upon a pedestalled statue, towering high by contrast with the lowliness around, and see the letters of Mozart's name flashing in the sunlight. Music, in "sculptured stone," is before me, bending with saddened face over the "Benedictus" of the master's *Requiem;* and an inscription tells all who care to read that this is Vienna's tribute to the illustrious child of Salzburg. It is too late, Vienna. Thou art right to seek a *locus penitentiæ;* but no tears can wash out the remembrance of thy sin, nor can votive offerings atone for it. When he who ranks among the greatest of all thy adopted sons was consigned here to the common grave—buried almost as a dog is buried—a deed was done never to be effaced. It is not even known for sure that the place of this monument is consecrated by his remains. But, though the reproach of Vienna endures, the matter may, after all, be well ordered. Mozart rose from the people, and to the people he has returned. His beautiful memorial towers above the "little crosses," to teach us that genius is independent alike of birth, of the accidents of life, and the utmost possible contumely of death. As though to show this more emphatically the poor graves literally crowd around

the monument. It cannot be said of the spot where the
master is thought to lie :—

> " It was a solitary mound,
> Which two spear's-lengths of level ground
> Did from all other graves divide,
> As if in some respect of pride."

Almost the nearest cross is that over the remains of a
mechanic, whose widow and children speak from the
inscription plate, in homely but touching verse, about the
void in their home. Less happy in death than even this
obscure workman was the illustrious composer. The
widow of Mozart, if she felt any sorrow at all, made no
public manifestation of it. "It was his attached servant
alone," says Nohl, "who thought of asking Constance
whether a cross should not be erected over the grave.
Her reply was that this was sure to be done, concluding
that the parish where the benediction took place would also
supply a cross. But subsequently, when she recovered,
and, her first burst of grief being over, she visited the
churchyard with her friends, there was a new sexton there
who could not point out the grave." So the resting-
place of genius remained unhonoured, till Vienna, in a
fit of penitence, erected the monument as near to it as
could be guessed.

Standing in the quiet cemetery, by the side of that
illustrious tomb, I fall to thinking how much the world
owes its dead occupant, and then I begin to wonder at

the fewness of the world's tokens of gratitude. All around me the graves of common men are loaded with offerings of affection; but on Mozart's memorial hang only two poor wreaths, long since faded and now dropping to pieces. It is clear that of those who for months past have visited the place not one has cared to leave behind a tribute of reverence and love. Had none of them in their heart a feeling akin to that which prompted Shakespeare's exquisite lines :—

> " With fairest flowers
> While summer lasts, and I live here, Fidele,
> I'll sweeten thy sad grave. Thou shalt not lack
> The flower that's like thy face, pale primrose ; nor
> The azured harebell, like thy veins ; no, nor
> The leaf of eglantine, which, not to slander,
> Outsweetened not thy breath : the ruddock would,
> With charitable bill, . . .
> . . . . bring thee all this ;
> Yea, and furred moss besides, when flowers are none,
> To winter-ground thy corse " ?

But it may be that the disproportion between the best possible offering and its object has stayed the else willing hand? Even if so, it shall not stay mine. Fortified by classic precedent, I do my best to " sweeten " Mozart's " sad grave " with " fairest flowers," and turn away from the spot as one leaves a solemn temple, " all reverence and fear."

Back to the busy streets of the city, and then once more I leave them behind, emerging now on the road by which the funeral trains of Beethoven and Schubert

passed to their destination—the historic cemetery of
Währing. Half a century ago Währing was really a
village, separated from Vienna by a wide space of open
country, and its burial-ground, though not connected
with any religious edifice, bore the character of a village
churchyard. It must have been a quiet pretty place
in those days, for even now, when the advancing capital
has thrown its arms about on all sides, a walk down
the main street reveals many a picturesque nook on
either hand as yet unreached by the march of improve-
ment. The street is full of quaint old houses, and not
even the life poured into it through the proximity of
upstart rivals can altogether dispel the air of congenial
repose. It was a happy thought to bury Beethoven at
Währing in the old ground over whose inclosing wall
ancient buildings gaze with appropriate sedateness of
aspect, and within hearing still of the sweet pastoral
noises that so often attuned his soul to harmony. As for
Schubert, we know that, even in delirium, his mind
dwelt upon the idea of resting near the greater master.
" I implore you," cried the dying man, " to carry me
to my room, and don't leave me in this corner under
the earth. What ! do I deserve no place above the
earth?" "Dear Franz, be calm," pleaded Ferdinand,
"you are in your own room—the same you always
had—and you are lying in your own bed." Then came

the answer, weak and querulous, but able to decide the
place of Schubert's rest. "No, it is not true; Beethoven
is not laid here." So it came to pass that the two, little
associated though they were in life, lie in death almost
side by side, only three graves separating their remains.

Passing up the village street, now well-nigh deserted
because of midday heat and glare, I come upon a
butcher lounging over the half-door of his little shop,
and him I ask as to the whereabouts of the cemetery.
In that butcher's mind the place is clearly associated
with a brewery, and through taking observation of a
brewery, under his direction, I find it out. The burial-
ground abuts upon the road, to which it presents a high
wall, with a gate flanked by the usual guardian's lodge.
I try the gate, but it is locked, and I fancy my pilgrimage
will end for this time in disappointment. Presently,
however, an old woman, bearing a watering-pot, crosses
the area of sunlit gravel within the archway, sees me
standing outside, and bids me enter through the lodge.
A moment after I pull just such another latch-string
as that which admitted Little Red Riding-Hood to her
grandmother's cottage, and am free of the inclosure.
The old woman, however, has had time enough to
disappear about her business; nor is there any one
else in all the place, as far as I can see, to
act as guide to the desired spot. So I proceed to

discover it by the exhaustive process, toiling up one
avenue and down another between battalions of tombs,
erected, if the inscriptions on them may be believed, to
the most virtuous people that death ever removed from
a world where virtue is sadly wanted.   There is so much
to exhaust that I am on the point of giving up the search
pro tem., when I see in the distance the outline of a
familiar head.   A minute afterwards I am standing by
the graves of the illustrious masters, impressed with the
situation and all its associations as none but those can
be to whom the masters themselves have acted, from
youth upwards, as cherished companions and a source
of unfailing delight.   The vaults are so placed that the
headstones rest against the boundary wall of the cemetery,
and in each case there is a little inclosure paved with
a ponderous stone, and surrounded by a low iron rail-
ing, within which admittance is gained by a gate.   I need
not remind the musical reader that the actual memorials
differ much from each other.   On Beethoven's, besides
the golden lyre and the serpent emblem of immortality,
there is nothing but the name of him whose mortal part
rests beneath; whereas Schubert's is adorned by a bust
of the master, and bears Grillparzer's inscription to the
well-remembered effect that "Death has here entombed a
rich treasure, but still more glorious hopes."   Between
the two stands a monument to a certain Graf O'Donnell,

one of the Irish soldiers of fortune who have never been
without representatives in the Austrian army. No doubt
the Graf was a potent man in his day, and perhaps
bespattered the musicians of Vienna with mud from his
charger's heels as he caracoled along the streets. But
—so true is it that Heaven is just, and that in the long
run all things find their level—Graf O'Donnell is only
known now because accident decided that his grave should
adjoin those of men who lived in poverty and affliction,
bearing no patent of nobility from King or Kaiser, and
not even having had the honour to be born, as birth is
understood in high and mighty circles.

> " Some, when they die, die all ; their mouldering clay
> Is but an emblem of their memories ;
> The space quite closes up through which they passed ; "

while others, not so honoured in life,—

> " Pluck the shining age from vulgar time
> And give it whole to late posterity."

As I stand musing before the tombs, a woman, armed
with a knife, comes up the avenue, opens the gate of
the Beethoven inclosure, and begins carefully to clip the
trailing plant that almost covers with perennial greenness
the recumbent stone. Then I notice with what attention
the grave and memorial are looked after. Then also
I observe with surprise and pain that the Schubert tomb
is falling into decay. Its plants are allowed to straggle
as they please ; the stonework is out of level and partially

ruinous; the fastening of the gate is broken, so that the
inclosure cannot be kept sacred, and, generally, the
appearance is that of a monument about which nobody
cares even to the extent of a few pounds a year.   Surely a
state of things so disgraceful to Vienna only needs pointing
out in order at once to be set right.   If not, then should
the admirers of Schubert belonging to the distant island
which was among the first of countries to acknowledge
his genius with a unanimous shout of admiration—then
should English amateurs go to the rescue and raise, as
they easily could, a small fund wherewith to keep the
tomb of their favourite in lasting repair.   Along with a
statement of the need for action I venture to give the
suggestion of a Schubert's Tomb Fund, and trust it may
not be wholly without result.

As I move reluctantly away from a spot so sacred and
from a scene that, once looked at, is permanently photo-
graphed on the brain, I meet a tourist, to all appearance
an American, carrying a red guidebook and closely scanning
the monuments on either hand.   Presently I turn and gaze
up the gentle slope of the avenue.   The American is
standing bareheaded before the tombs, his white hair
glistening in the sunlight as though it reflected some of
the glory of the masters.   Ever since I have accepted that
motionless figure as part of the picture—the world through
him offering homage at the shrine of genius.

A SUPPER WITH WAGNER.

HAD the Bayreuth Festival taken place in England it is
tolerably certain that the official arrangements would have
comprised a dinner, with a lord in the chair, and a toast-
master behind him, the " usual loyal and patriotic toasts,"
in addition to that " of the evening," and any number of
speeches, from the oration of Wagner himself down to
the stammering utterance of the retired Rear-Admiral
who is always telling us that " the Navy, my lord, will,
if called upon, I can assure your lordship, do its duty
as in former times." But as the Festival happened in
Germany, the idea of a feast other than that of reason,
and a flow other than that of soul, was left about for
any one to pick up who chose. Naturally, the pro-
prietor of the *Restauration* attached to the Wagner
theatre seized upon it, with a tradesmanlike view to
profit, as well as, no doubt, a commendable desire to unite
the master and his disciples under pleasant circumstances. Wagner agreeing that this should be, the theatre
was one day bespotted with handbills emanating from the

spirited caterer, who desired all and sundry to note that for five marks of the realm the honour of a supper with the great man could be obtained. I paid five marks and enjoyed the distinction, which was certainly cheap at the price.

It was an "off-day" of the Festival, when one might have been excused for lolling in the shade of a *Bier-garten*, trying to clear one's throat of accumulated dust, or anticipating the delight of the happy hour when next the eye would rest upon a well-spread English dinner-table—food in Bayreuth was only to be had by skilful foraging. But one could not yield to this temptation and also sup with Wagner—fancy supper at five o'clock or thereabouts!—so once more I dragged wearily along the blinding choking road that led to the scene of operations, passing as I did so the squirt upon wheels which the corporate intellect of Bayreuth had previously determined was a watering-cart of sufficient dimensions. A motley throng gradually whitened themselves with me along that *viâ dolorosa*—enthusiastic Yankee ladies, in a chronic state of ecstasy about "darling Liszt," whose shadow they hoped would fall upon them by-and-by; wild-looking Germans of various types, bound by the common bond of long hair and spectacles; unbelieving Frenchmen, always keeping together, as though for mutual assistance, and always meditating epigrams of a withering character;

and English pilgrims not a few, looking at one another askance, as who should say, " If you don't agree with me about this business take care when I catch you at home." One after another, or in straggling groups, we gained the Wagnerian inclosure, pulled ourselves up the gentle ascent, and sank to rest in the open balconies of the refreshment buildings. Inside preparations were making for many guests; but the resources of the establishment were not taxed to the degree one might have expected. The sanguine eye had seen visions of the whole town-full of visitors, to say nothing of the town itself, rushing pell-mell to the supper-tables. But the reality came short of the dream, and only some four or five hundred thought the honour worth its cost. The rest were wrong.

A blazing sun, like that in the " Ancient Mariner," drooped over the distant town as we were permitted to enter the supper-room and seek our places. Let me here describe the arrangement of the tables, asking the reader to imagine the nave of a church, having at one end a transept sunk six feet or more below the level. The transept was the place of honour. There, at tables seating some dozen guests each, were placed the visitors of distinction, and indeed most of those who had come from foreign lands. On the higher floor of the nave were ranged other tables stretching along its whole length, the centre one devoted to artists and persons connected with

the theatre. It followed, of course, that the guests in the
nave were for the most part out of sight of those in the
transept, and *vice versâ;* but the arrangement quite
harmonised with proceedings marked generally by a
delightful absence of rule and order. The chief place of
honour was at the table immediately facing the steps
leading down from nave to transept, and round this
soon gathered a group amid which the striking figure
of Liszt was prominent. Madame Wagner, too, was
there, and naturally the "Master" also: but he had
taken a resolution. Rejecting the distinguished place
assigned him, and preferring to be with his artists,
he mounted the steps and moved to the head of
the centre table in the nave, amid loud applause.
The *coup* met with the success it deserved, and the
American ladies near me had such an aggravation of
ecstasy as could only be relieved by copious notes in
dainty pocket-books. At length all was ready, and at the
sound of a bell out filed a little army of waiters with the
first of the curious "courses" that make up a German
repast. Englishmen who are unacquainted with the
fashions of their Teutonic relatives on such occasions, and
who know only that among themselves the feeding process is solemn enough to go on undisturbed, will scarcely
be prepared for the information that at Bayreuth we
took bodily and mental refreshment in alternate layers.

Sandwichlike, a speech came between two dishes, and a
dish between two speeches or more, for as enthusiasm
warmed the *cacoëthes loquendi* prevailed.   The effect upon
our supper, I am bound to add, was not happy.   With
such hunger as characterised life in Bayreuth only half ap-
peased, it was provoking—I put it feelingly to the average
Englishman—to see dishes cooling in the hands of the
waiters, who dared not serve them till some long-winded
orator chose to sit down.   But worse still remains to be
told.   It is sometimes said that no half-dozen Anglo-
Saxons can meet together without electing a chairman
and putting themselves under government :—

> " So work the honey-bees,
> Creatures that by a rule in nature teach
> The act of order to a peopled kingdom."

But on this occasion there was no order, and every man did
what was right in his own eyes.   As at a Quaker's meeting,
those who were moved to speak spoke, when they could
get the chance; and it was simply owing to the modesty
or self-restraint of the guests that a score were not
haranguing their neighbours at the same moment.   How
much of the proceedings therefore was either comical
or aggravating, according as the unaccustomed spectator
chose to regard it, I need not stop to tell.   The interest
of the evening really began when a gentleman of
distinguished bearing, a member, I am told, of the

Hungarian Parliament, solemnly advanced to the foot of the steps leading to the nave and began a set speech in praise of Wagner. He at once commanded attention. The guests above left their tables and crowded to see the speaker, while the master himself posed in the midst of them, gravely listening to the details of his own transcendent merits. The Hungarian, if such in truth he was, did his work well. He had a good voice, the manner of an orator, a fluent delivery, and the art of adapting himself to his audience, so that every one seemed to be hearing the expression of his own thoughts. Moreover he worked up to a striking peroration, in which, pointing to Wagner, he spoke of the poet-composer as another Siegfried, who had "rode the flaming fire" to wake the Brünnhilde of art with a kiss. Of course the trope, calmly looked at, strikes us as utter nonsense, because Siegfried-Wagner, whatever fire he may have gone through, found Brünnhilde as broad awake as was the Walkyrie maiden when the sham Gunther stole upon her. But the purpose of the time was served. The parable sent its hearers into ecstasies, the Yankee ladies made "a note on't" diligently enough to have delighted the soul of Cap'en Ed'ard Cuttle, and Siegfried-Wagner was moved to descend the steps, throw himself on the orator's neck, and kiss his cheek with effusion. After this we all threw ourselves on the ice-creams.

But the "game," using the term without irreverence, had only just begun. The big guns were yet to come into action, and the biggest of all was the first to open fire. Wagner, once more posing on the top of the steps, with his body-guard around him, delivered a speech. He is no orator. His manner lacks grace, and his words do not flow freely. Yet there is something about him that would dispose one to listen, even if his claim upon attention were unknown. His words on this occasion were not offensively marked by the assumption of superiority which necessarily belongs to a man who pretends to reform where others think no reform necessary. He even condescended to explain a previous utterance, which, having been misinterpreted, had given offence. "You have now an art," said Wagner to the Germans in the theatre. The words naturally rankled into wounds, and men began sorely to cry out, "What, had we no art before the *Nibelungen?*" At the supper we learned that Wagner really intended to say, "You have now a *new* art;" and the explanation, coming from such a quarter, was no doubt a condescension to be prized. But Wagner, gracious beyond himself, actually spoke of the national opera of France and Italy without a sneer; not only so, he admitted that the forms of art in question were suited to the genius of their respective nations. This was not Siegfried in the Ercles vein—not Siegfried luring the dragon from his hole that Nothung, "conquering sword," might be fleshed—but rather Siegfried in the gentle shepherd mood, making a pipe to imitate the little birds. Wagner was all that evening in the gentle shepherd mood. Corydon is sometimes crowned with a wreath woven by the hands of Phillis, and even the wreath was not wanting to the Corydon of our supper-table. Phillis, in the person of Signora Lucca, publisher of the master's works for Italy, took a wreath—appropriately made of artificial leaves—and as Wagner passed deftly clapped it on his head. He wore it. Let the fact go forth to all who fancy that the terrible Richard breathes nothing but fire and smoke, like Fafner the "Worm." He, laughing, wore the Luccese wreath during his promenade among the guests, and entered into the fun of the incident with all the zest of a boy. It was a happy moment for the master, and no doubt a happy moment for Signora Lucca :—

> " Quid dedicatum posoit Apollinem
> vates ? quid orat de paterâ novum
> fundens liquorem ? "

But the crowning incident of the evening was the Wagner-Liszt episode. Here let me speak in terms of studied respect. To English eyes the sight of two elderly gentlemen embracing and mingling their tears in public seems odd, but not even Lord Palmerston's *civis Romanus* has a right to expect the whole world to act upon his notion of what is fitting. The males of the Germanic race have no objection to kiss each other, and on German ground there was not the smallest reason why Liszt and Wagner, after sounding each other's praises with ten-trumpet power, should not fall on each other's bosom. At all events they did it, and twice. First Wagner, from the eminence of the steps, spoke of Liszt, who rose and faced the orator. Embrace No. 1 followed. Next, having given his son-in-law time to remount the steps, Liszt spoke of Wagner; after which came embrace No. 2, the assembly meanwhile expressing the liveliest satisfaction. Very funny to the British eye was all this, but no possessor of the optic in question had a right to utter his favourite ejaculation, "humbug!" The distinguished actors were doubtless perfectly sincere. During long years, through evil and through good, they had remained true to a common friendship, based on mutual admiration and sympathy, and both had now reached the goal of many hopes, the end of arduous labour, the consummation of many wishes. The occasion was therefore one of extraordinary interest, and before all who cared to look on they showed how deeply it touched them. But such a high-strung condition of things could not last long, and Wagner ended it by exclaiming, "Now let us have no more serious business!"

Here the interest of my story ends, for the reader would

probably fail to appreciate the heavy forms of humour in which merry-minded Germans indulge. Enough that the festivity went on, and that the feasters—some of them—might have been seen and heard at the principal *Bierhalle* of the town—well, perhaps I had better not say how many hours afterwards.

INDEX.

APPENDIX.

NOVELLO, EWER AND CO.,

Printers,

69 & 70, Dean Street, Soho, London, W.

www.ingramcontent.com/pod-product-compliance
Lightning Source LLC
Chambersburg PA
CBHW020017030726
47500CB00002B/634